A

Little Rain

Must Fall

Ted and Audrey
Summer Lake Silver Book Three

By SJ McCoy

A Sweet n Steamy Romance

Published by Xenion, Inc

Published by Xenion, Inc.
First paperback edition 2020
www.sjmccoy.com

This book is a work of fiction. Names, characters, places, and events are figments of the author's imagination, fictitious, or are used fictitiously. Any resemblance to actual events, locales or persons living or dead is coincidental.

Cover Design by Dana Lamothe of Designs by Dana
Editor: Mitzi Pummer Carroll
Proofreaders: Aileen Blomberg, Marisa Nichols, Traci Atkinson.

ISBN: 978-1-946220-67-7

Dedication

For Sam. Sometimes, life really is too short. Few.

xxx

Chapter One

Audrey checked the mirror on the back of the door before she opened it. Ugh. She normally wouldn't set foot out in public looking like this. Her hair was pulled up into a messy bun, her eyes gave away the fact that she'd only had a few hours' sleep, and her sweat suit wasn't going to fool anyone into thinking that she was on her way to an early morning workout at the hotel gym.

Oh well. She made a face at herself, which at least brought a smile. She was a woman with priorities. And her priority at this moment was coffee. She didn't understand why otherwise wonderful hotels such as this only provided two cups' worth. It wasn't their fault, she reminded herself as she opened the door and stepped out into the hallway. She was fully aware of the situation and normally carried her own supplies. She could picture her travel pack of Peet's sitting on the counter at home. She'd had it all ready to pack, but then Izzy had shown up, and in her usual whirlwind fashion had hurried Audrey out, chiding her that she didn't need to over-prepare.

She stabbed at the button to summon the elevator. Izzy would no doubt be sleeping blissfully for another few hours. She stepped into the elevator and rode down to the lobby. It was only five-twenty, but there had to be fresh coffee around somewhere. And if there wasn't, she'd find someone to make some, or if all else failed, drive until she found a convenience store!

The girl at the front desk greeted her with a cheery smile. "Good morning."

"Morning." Audrey was still reserving judgment about whether it qualified as good. "Where can I get coffee?"

"The dining room doesn't open for a little while yet, but—"

Audrey felt her lips press together.

The girl smiled. "But I just brewed a fresh pot. I'll bring it out."

Audrey smiled back at her. "You're an angel."

She laughed. "No. Angel's the general manager; I'm Roxy."

She went into the office and came back out pushing a cart with the promised pot of coffee and a jug of cream and sugar packets and all the other unnecessary things people used to contaminate their caffeine.

Audrey poured herself a mug and breathed in before she took a sip.

"Do you need—?"

She shook her head. "I have what I need."

Roxy laughed. "In that case, I'll be quiet. I think silence is one of the most important accompaniments to the first cup of the day."

Audrey smiled. "You're good, Roxy. I'll find you to thank you properly when I'm feeling more human. When are you on again?"

"Not until Monday. I don't normally work nights anymore; I'm just covering."

"Well, I hope you enjoy your weekend, and I'll see you Monday. I'm here for the week."

"I'll look forward to it. Enjoy your coffee and have a lovely stay. But …" Roxy frowned and held up a finger, implying Audrey should wait while she went back into the office. She returned with a travel mug and filled it up. Then she put the lid on and handed it over along with a bag containing several of the coffee pods for the in-room coffee maker. "You can give the mug back to me on Monday."

"I say again, you're an angel."

The phone rang and Roxy gave her an apologetic shrug. Audrey was happy to leave her to get on with it.

Instead of heading straight back to the elevator, she wandered around the ground floor. She liked to get her bearings wherever she stayed, but Izzy had been in such a hurry to drop their things in their rooms and then get out and look around when they'd arrived last night that she hadn't had time to explore the lodge.

She stuck her head around the door of the business center. Hopefully, she wouldn't need to use it, but knowing her, she would. It surprised her; it looked as though it had everything a person could need, and yet, it didn't feel sterile or even office like.

She smiled to herself as she closed the door and took another sip of her coffee before continuing on to take a look at the workout room. She didn't have any great expectations, and it wasn't an issue. If there was an elliptical, she'd be happy. She'd brought her mat and could do yoga in her room. She stopped at the glass door and was impressed by what she saw. There was all the standard gym equipment and more: a row of ellipticals, stationary bikes, treadmills, and rowing machines. There were also free weights and benches and a matted area large enough for group classes. She nodded to herself and took another drink of her coffee.

She almost choked on it when she realized that she was smiling and nodding through the door, and that a man was sitting pedaling away on one of the bikes, smiling back at her. It was amazing how the mind only saw what it expected to. She'd expected the place to be empty, so hadn't noticed him sitting there in plain sight—no doubt watching her as she gawked and nodded to herself!

She forced herself to smile politely back at him and as she did, she wondered how she could have missed him before. A little shiver ran down her spine. She'd always had a thing for guys who worked out—more because of what it said about their personality than what it did for them physically. Though, she couldn't deny that had its benefits—especially in his case.

Her gaze locked with his, sending more shivers down her spine. He was older—older than her, even, and that was saying something. But there was a vitality about him—in his eyes— not just in the way his muscled legs pumped the pedals. She had to reel her wayward imagination in before it could go off and play with ideas of his muscular legs ... and arms ... and him pumping ...

She raised her mug to him before turning away and hurrying back to the elevator. Maybe Izzy was right. Maybe she needed to start dating again. It'd been a long time since she'd been with a man. She'd thought that Richard might have put her off for life but, she smiled to herself as she stepped into the elevator, she had a feeling that the guy in the gym could persuade her to change her mind if he were so inclined.

Ted sucked in big breath of fresh air. It felt so good. There was something about the air up here that was unlike anything he'd experienced anywhere else. It smelled of pine and mountains, but he wouldn't describe it as mountain air.

Something about the lake made it different. He lifted his gaze and looked out at the lake as he made his way down the path to the shore. This had become his routine whenever he came here—his early morning workout in the lodge's gym, followed by a shower and a light breakfast at the café in the plaza and then this treat—his walk on the beach.

It would be more convenient to stay on the other side of the lake, at the resort. That'd be closer to his son, Eddie. But he didn't want to be on their doorstep. He was so grateful that Eddie and April had allowed him into their life to the extent that they had. He knew he didn't deserve it, and he didn't want to overstep any boundaries. He went to their house whenever they invited him. He hung out with his grandson, Marcus, as much as possible. He smiled to himself. Technically, Marcus wasn't his grandson; he was April's child, not Eddie's—at least, not by birth. But to Marcus, and to him, he was Granddad. And that was all that mattered.

He pulled his cell phone out of his back pocket when it rang and answered without even checking the display. It was seven in the morning; his partner called him at this time every day.

"Buenos días, mi amigo."

Diego laughed. "Good morning, to you. I take it you slept well, and are out for your walk?"

"That's right. How about you?"

"I've done my work for the day. Now I get to hang out with Zack until Maria finishes work."

"That's good." Diego and his son Zack had been estranged for many years. Not as long as Ted and Eddie, and for very different reasons, but Ted was glad that his friend was enjoying being part of family life now in the same way that he was.

"I think so. And you?"

"I'm waiting to hear what the plan is for the day."

"Will I see you at the Boathouse this evening?"

"I think so. Eddie said that it'll be very busy tonight because they have a big party. I don't like that idea, but I do love to see him play."

"We can find a quiet spot at the end of the bar, I'm sure. We can sit and drink like the pair of old farts that we are."

Ted had to laugh. "Because of course, you're such a quiet and reserved character and sitting quietly at the end of the bar is your idea of fun."

Diego laughed with him. "Or perhaps, I'm only trying to make it sound more appealing to you. I'm going, but I don't want to hang myself around the young people's necks. I'd rather see what mischief we can get into."

Ted pursed his lips. Diego loved his mischief as he called it. He loved the ladies—and they loved him. The two of them still had a lot of fun, at home in Orange County. It was different here, though. Here at Summer Lake, he wanted to be the father and grandfather who his son could respect—not chase women with Diego.

Diego sighed. "Okay. Okay. I'll behave. We shall be the respectable, older generation—but you owe me a night out when we go home."

Ted laughed. "Deal. You know I don't want to spoil your fun, it's just …"

"No need to explain, Edward. No need. We want to be men they can look up to, not degenerates they're embarrassed by."

"Something like that. Anyway, do you have anything interesting to tell me on the work front?"

"All quiet. Everything is as it should be. No surprises. We're good to relax until Monday."

"I'm glad to hear it. I'll check in with you later."

"And I'll see you at the Boathouse, if not before."

"Okay. See you then."

He put his phone back into his pocket and shrugged a little deeper into his jacket. Spring was in the air, but it was still colder here than at home. He caught a glimpse of movement in the sky and looked up to see an eagle flying overhead. It made him smile. It made him want to stay here. This was a good place. Laguna Beach wasn't a bad place—far from it. It was the kind of place that said you'd made it, and Ted knew that he had. But he wasn't even sure what that term meant to him anymore. He'd made it financially—more than made it. But what did that really mean? He turned and started back toward the lodge, fully aware that that was the kind of question you could only ponder once you were there.

He'd spent years of his life—decades—pursuing success. Now he had it, and he was proud of himself, proud of all he'd achieved. But more and more lately, he stopped to wonder what it was all worth. He knew that, given the choice, he'd trade it all and come and live here simply, close to his son and the boy he called his grandson.

~ ~ ~

"Oh, look at you!" Izzy exclaimed when she opened her door to Audrey. "Let me guess. You've been up since the crack of sparrow fart, working?"

Audrey laughed. "I woke up early, yes. But I've not been working. I took a little walk."

Izzy shuddered as she led her into the room. "Saturday mornings are for sleeping in and relaxing."

"Taking a walk is relaxing for me."

"True. At least you're not working. That's something."

"I thought you might be proud of me."

Izzy went and flopped down on the unmade bed. "Sorry. I am. I just want to see you relaxed and happy."

"I am. If you judge by my standards and not yours."

Izzy gave her a rueful smile. "Are you trying to tell me that I have low standards?"

"I wouldn't dare. Though, if I were to imply such a thing, I might bring up Rafa as an example."

Izzy threw a pillow at her and laughed. "I wondered how long it'd take. You're right, of course. If I were trying to uphold some kind of standard, then I would never allow Rafa to darken my door. But, sweet Audrey, I'm not. I'm just having a little fun. If you could learn to do the same …"

Audrey blew out a sigh. "You know full well, I'm not into—"

"I didn't mean if you could learn to bonk your personal trainer!" Izzy laughed. "I've given up on trying to get you interested in the male of the species. I just meant if you could learn to have a little fun."

"Sorry. I didn't mean to jump down your throat. And to tell you the truth …"

"What?"

"Nothing. Well, actually, no. I'll tell you. You shouldn't give up on me and men. I was thinking about that this morning. Thinking that maybe you're right."

Izzy's eyes widened and she leaned forward eagerly. "And what made you think about that? You shut me down whenever I try to."

Audrey couldn't hide her smile. "Don't laugh at me. You'll think it's pathetic. But I went downstairs this morning in search of coffee. I was checking the place out—"

"As you do."

"Yes. And I went to look at the workout room."

"Ooh! And you saw a hot, young body you'd like to work out with?"

Audrey had to laugh. "You're so bad. I saw a very attractive man. But, no, he wasn't a young body."

Izzy's smile faded. "I've told you; you don't have to resign yourself to men our age and older, you know. We're living in the modern age—this is the era of the cougar. As long as you're in decent shape—and you're in great shape—the younger guys are all about it."

"Do you want me tell you or not?"

Izzy laughed. "Yes. Sorry, go on. What was he like? What happened?"

"He was … I don't know … sexy … in a very manly way." She didn't miss the expression on her friend's face. "Don't look at me like that. I don't know how else to say it. I know you like them younger, and that's fine for you. But I appreciate a real man."

"And you don't think Rafa's a real man?" She waggled her eyebrows.

"Of course, I do. In a testosterone-driven, young buck kind of way. This guy was obviously older, still in great shape and … I don't know how to describe it, but I don't suppose it matters. It's not about him; it's about the effect he had on me. He sent shivers down my spine—reminded me how that felt. I suppose you could say that he woke something in me, something that I thought had died after the divorce, but apparently, it was only dormant."

For once, Izzy looked serious. "That's wonderful, Audrey. I want to find him and—"

"Didn't you hear me? It's not about him."

"Give me a chance? I want to find him and thank him for doing something that I haven't been able to."

"What's that?"

"Reminding you that you're still a woman. A beautiful, sensual woman."

Audrey smiled. "I don't know about that, but thank you."

"You are beautiful, you know."

"Of course, I am. Every woman is beautiful in her own way."

"I don't just mean the feelgood crap we spout to make ourselves feel better. I mean in an objective way. You're a beautiful woman."

Audrey stared out of the window for a few moments before looking back at her friend. "Thank you. Richard ... the way things went ... it made me feel ..." She didn't know how to put it into words, and she wasn't sure she even wanted to.

She should have remembered that she didn't need to. Izzy scowled the way she did whenever Richard's name came up. "You know what I think of him, so I won't go there. What I will say is that after what he did, it's no surprise that you stopped seeing yourself as desirable and beautiful. But honestly, Audrey, it's time for you to get over it, and I think this weekend is the perfect chance."

Audrey made a face. "I wish he wasn't coming."

"Or that he had the decency not to bring *her*."

Audrey shrugged. "She's his wife now. He's hardly going to leave her at home, is he?"

Izzy opened her mouth, but then closed it again quickly.

She didn't need to say the words. Audrey knew she was about to remind her that he'd left her at home often enough in all the years they'd been married—and especially the last few.

"Anyway. Let's not think about him before we have to. What's happening today? Are we doing anything with the kids or just meeting up with them tonight?"

"I told Ally to call me if there's anything I can do, but other than that, we'll just see them tonight."

Izzy nodded, and Audrey knew that she was feeling sorry for her.

She smiled brightly. "Don't look like that. It's their thirtieth birthday. I'm happy that they want me here at all. I'm happy that they're still so close that they want a joint birthday party."

"I know. It's wonderful, and we should focus on that. It's better than them expecting you to organize it all for them. This way we're free to spend the day doing whatever we please. I'd love to explore the shopping plaza. I read that there's a wonderful clothing store—Hayes—over there. Maybe we can find you a gorgeous dress to wear tonight—something that'll make you feel beautiful."

"Maybe we should. I brought a nice black dress with me."

Izzy rolled her eyes. "No comment. But can we at least go and take a poke around in Hayes? There might be something that's perfect. And you never know, we might run into your sexy old man from the gym."

Audrey had to laugh. "I didn't say he was an old man."

"Sorry. Yes. Older, not old."

Audrey nodded. She didn't need to say it. It hung in the air; the stark contrast between her being attracted to an older man and Richard now being married to a much younger woman.

Chapter Two

"Do you really have to go home tomorrow, Grandad?"

Ted pursed his lips. He found it hard to say no to Marcus.

April gave the boy a stern look. "Don't pester. You know Grandad has to go back to work. And you'll be at school anyway. You can't expect him to hang around all day waiting for you." She smiled at Ted. "Though you know he's not the only one who loves having you here."

"And you know I love being here." He was already wondering if there was any reason he shouldn't take a few days off. It wasn't as though he needed to be in the office every day. He was more of a figure-head these days. "I don't want to interrupt your routines, though."

April raised an eyebrow at him. "I'm not saying we wouldn't love for you to stay." She looked at Marcus. "I just don't want him twisting your arm."

Marcus laughed. "You don't need to worry about that, Mom. Grandad's too smart for me. You're about the only one whose arm I can twist anymore."

Ted had to chuckle. The boy was right. April was a kind soul. She'd had a tough time before she met Eddie, and she was very protective of Marcus.

"Don't bank on being able to twist mine anymore, young man. I'm getting wise to you."

He went and wrapped his arms around her waist. "I'm only playing."

They all looked up when Eddie came in through the front door. "Sorry, that took longer than I expected." He checked his watch. "Is everyone ready?"

"Ready and waiting," said Marcus.

Eddie punched his shoulder. "Watch it, lil dude."

Ted loved the way the boy smiled back at him and said, "Sorry, Dad." It filled his heart up to watch the two of them together. It was bittersweet for him. He loved that Eddie and Marcus had formed such a strong bond, they had so much love for each other. At the same time, it saddened him that he hadn't been there for most of Eddie's childhood. He was so grateful for the relationship they had now, but it could never make up for all the years he'd lost. He'd been a fool, and he knew it.

Eddie turned to him. "Ready?"

He nodded. He was looking forward to getting out on the lake. He'd taught Eddie to fish when he was a kid, and it made him happy that they got to share it again now with Marcus.

Once they were out on the lake, Eddie turned to him with a smile. "I know it's not like your boat, but this is all right, don't you think?"

Ted smiled. "It's more than all right, son. I love it." He jerked his head to where Marcus was sitting with April fishing off the stern. "And you know they do."

"We've got a good little life going here."

"I wouldn't call it a little life."

Eddie shrugged. "You know what I mean. It's just a simple life. I'm not out making big money or doing anything significant in the world. But I'm happy—and so are they."

"That's the biggest thing there is: being happy. Making your family happy is much more important than making money. I only wish I'd understood that sooner."

"I'm just glad we figured it out before it was too late."

Ted nodded and looked out at the lake. The years he'd lost with Eddie were the biggest regret of his life.

Eddie punched his arm. "Of course, I'd go back and change the past if I could. But today is the only time we can make anything happen; we can't change yesterday, and we can't live for tomorrow."

"So much wiser than your father." Ted gave him a rueful smile.

Eddie laughed. "Not wiser—though it seems I have a better memory. You were the one who told me that when I was just a little kid."

"Dad, will you see if you can get Grandad to stay?" called Marcus.

Eddie raised an eyebrow at him. "What's that about?"

"He asked earlier if I have to go home tomorrow."

Eddie turned and called back to Marcus. "Grandad's got to work, dude. You know that."

"Would I be in the way?"

"Hell, no! We'd all love it if you wanted to stick around a bit longer. I just try not to get too greedy about hogging your time."

"I …" Ted had to clear his throat before he could go on. "I love spending time with you. You know that. And as I said earlier, family is so much more important than work."

Eddie grinned. "So, stay, why don't you? If it were up to me, I'd ask you to move here, stay full-time."

Ted's breath caught in chest. "You would?"

"Yeah. I know you won't, but that's not the reason I'm saying it. I need you to know. That's how far we've come."

Ted swallowed—hard.

Marcus came and popped his head into the cabin where they were sitting. "When can you come back?"

Ted looked at Eddie before he answered. "It turns out, I can stay a little longer."

"Awesome!" He turned and called to April. "Grandad's going to stay a while, Mom!"

April came to join them. Ted was very pleasantly surprised by how happy she looked. "That's great news!"

"You don't mind?"

She made a face at him. "I have the best father-in-law in the world; why would I mind that we get to keep him for a little longer?"

"He's not really your father-in-law though, is he?" asked Marcus. "Just like he's not really my Grandad. He won't be until you guys get married."

Ted tried to hide his smile. He knew that Eddie wanted them to get married more than anything in the world. April did, too. But she'd had a rough go with her divorce and hadn't wanted to go straight back into another marriage. She loved Eddie with all her heart; he didn't doubt that. It was just that she'd wanted to be right with herself before she became his wife. Ted respected that about her. She was a kind soul, soft-hearted, but she'd grown so much and become so much stronger in the time Ted had known her. Eddie and Marcus were impatient for them to finally tie the knot, but Ted respected that April had taken her time.

"We're working on it."

Judging by the look on her face, Ted guessed that she was just as eager as her son to finally make it happen.

Eddie ruffled the boy's hair. "I've told you. This year. It's going to happen, okay?"

Marcus batted Eddie's hand away and grinned at Ted. "I know. I just like to keep reminding you both."

"Did you know that Clay McAdam lives here?" asked Izzy.

"Of course, I did. You told me all about it when the kids first decided to hold their party here. To be honest, I thought that was the reason you were so excited to come."

Izzy gave her a hurt look. "That's not fair. I know I chatter on about sexy men more than I should. But do you really think that's more important to me than being here for Ally and Brayden's birthday? We've been best friends forever, Audrey.

I'm the twins' godmother. I'm thrilled that they thought to invite me."

Audrey felt bad. "Sorry, I didn't mean anything by it."

Izzy picked up her card and left a twenty as a tip. "Come on. Let's go and have a wander around the stores shall we. This plaza may be the best kept shopping secret I've ever discovered. Hayes is here, and did you know that Laura Hamilton has a store here, too?"

"That I did know. Shall we go and have a look? I love her jewelry."

"As if I'm going to say no. Let's stop in Hayes first, though. And if we can find you a knockout dress to wear tonight, I'm buying it for you."

Audrey laughed. "You hated the black one that much?"

Izzy linked arms with her as they left the café. "I didn't hate it. It's perfectly fine—if you're going to a funeral."

Audrey had to laugh. "Thanks."

"I'm only teasing. It's a nice dress. But you deserve to wear a fantastic dress—especially tonight."

Audrey's smile faded. "Thanks. I'm dreading it, you know."

"I do know. I hate it for you. Richard's an asshole and Natalee—"

Audrey held a hand up to stop her. "Don't. She seems nice enough. I don't want to turn into the bitter old ex who's jealous of the pretty young wife who he replaced me with. I just feel old and frumpy and a little bit sad. I'm not sure I could get through this evening without you."

Izzy squeezed her arm. "You don't have to. I'm here for you. I've got your back." They'd reached Hayes now and Izzy stopped before they went in. "I know you feel sad, and I'm doing everything I can to make you feel better. You might feel old, but you're not." She smiled. "You're two months and two days younger than me. So, I get offended when you say you're old. And the frumpy thing? You might have a point there, but that's an easy fix. That's what we're here for." She pushed the door open and gestured for Audrey to go in ahead of her.

It was a beautiful store. Audrey looked around in wonder. There were so many lovely clothes and shoes and jewelry. There was a nice feel to the place, too. She often felt uncomfortable in clothing stores—either too old or too frumpy. This place made her feel—not quite at home, but as though she'd like to fit in here.

"Ladies. Welcome!" A guy came bustling toward them with a big smile. He clasped his hands together and let his gaze travel over first Audrey and then Izzy. Audrey felt as though it should make her uncomfortable, but it didn't. It made her stand a little straighter and want to be worthy of his scrutiny.

"Welcome to Hayes. I'm Roberto. What can I do for you?"

"Oh, my goodness!" exclaimed Izzy. "Roberto? I thought you worked in the LA store. You're a legend!"

Roberto beamed at her and swatted the air with his hand. "Well, aren't you a sweetheart? This is your lucky day. I'm up here visiting Holly, and I just couldn't resist coming in and seeing what kind of clientele visits us here. I have to say, I'm impressed so far."

Audrey laughed. She liked him a lot. He was way over the top, but his smile was genuine, and his manner was warm and welcoming.

Izzy reached out to shake his hand. "I'm Izzy, and this is Audrey. And you have made our weekend by being here."

"Not yet, I haven't. But tell me what you're looking for, and I'll see what I can do. My mission is to help you find something that will make you feel as fabulous as you are."

Izzy grinned at Audrey. "You don't know how lucky we are. I wasn't joking. Roberto's a legend. He's exactly what you need."

Roberto turned to her. "We're shopping for you? And what is it that you think you need?"

"A dress. I have a party this evening."

"I see. Formal? Casual? Somewhere in between? How do you want to feel?"

Audrey stared at him. "It's definitely not formal. It's a birthday party for my children—they're twins. It's at the Boathouse; do you know it?"

"I do. Do you need something practical?"

She sensed a hint of distaste in his tone that she didn't understand.

"If you're going to be dealing with hordes of small children?"

She laughed out loud. "No! There won't be any small children. It's their thirtieth birthday."

"Thirtieth?" He looked incredulous. And if he was faking it, he did a very good job. "Your children are thirty? Darling, there's no way you're old enough!"

"Believe me. I'm old enough."

"She doesn't look it, does she?" Izzy smiled at Roberto. "The trouble is, she feels it, and that's what we need your help with."

"I'm your man. So, what's your style? I see you as the embodiment of grace and elegance. Do you want to feel regal?"

Audrey nodded; she liked the sound of that. "I'd hardly call myself elegant—utilitarian is more my style, but I'd like to step it up a notch tonight."

Roberto smiled and Audrey didn't miss the way he checked out her wedding finger. "Are you taking a date?"

"No."

Izzy blew out a sigh. "Do you mind if I tell him the situation?"

"Okay." Audrey wasn't sure that she wanted Izzy telling her sad tale to a stranger, but Roberto seemed like a decent person, and if the information could help him to better understand how she wanted to feel in whatever she wore tonight, then why not?

Roberto leaned forward eagerly with a conspiratorial smile. "Spill the beans, Izzy. What's the situation?"

"Well, with it being the kids' birthday party, they've invited their father, too—and his new wife."

Roberto curled his lip. "And we don't like her?"

"She's all right," said Audrey. "It's not her fault."

"Pft!" Izzy made a face.

"It's not," Audrey insisted. "She can't help that she's twenty years younger than me." She shrugged at Roberto. "It's not her fault that I feel old and frumpy."

Roberto took her arm and started leading her toward the back of the store. "Let's talk colors. I'm going to pick you out a few things to try so I can get an idea of what will work for you. By the time I'm done with you, horrible him—the man you were once married to—will be wondering why he ever let you go. And little miss new knickers will be completely eclipsed while you dazzle everyone."

Audrey chuckled. "You have great faith in your ability to make silk purses out of sow's ears, then?"

Roberto frowned. "You are no sow's ear. A diamond in the rough, perhaps." He winked. "And as for my abilities, you should listen to Izzy—I'm a legend for a reason!"

~ ~ ~

"Hey, Ted." Kenzie, the bartender greeted him with a smile. "It's good to see you. Are you just hanging with Eddie while they get set up, or are you here for the night?"

"I'm here for as much of the night as I can stand. I understand you're in for a busy one?"

"We are. There's a big birthday party coming in. We'd normally use upstairs for that, but they know a lot of people here, and they wanted to do it down here. It's going to be nuts. But you have to get the time with Eddie while you can, right?"

Ted looked up at the stage where Eddie was setting up the equipment with Kenzie's husband Chase. The two of them had been best friends for many years. "That's the theory, but I might just dip out early. Crowds aren't my thing. I love to see them play, but ..."

"I hear ya. I love to listen to them, too. But it's not the same when I'm back here. Oh, look. Here's Diego."

Diego came and took a seat next to Ted.

"What can I get you guys?"

"Just a Coke for me, thanks," said Ted.

Diego rolled his eyes. "Out to have a wild time, then?"

Kenzie laughed. "You leave him alone. I'm guessing you want your Remy?"

Diego smiled at her. "You know me so well."

Ted smirked as she went to get their drinks. Diego charmed every woman he met, no matter how old or young or married she might be. "Where's Zack?"

"They're coming a little later. I said I'd meet them here. Is April coming?"

"No. She's staying home with Marcus tonight. He has a friend over. And I don't think she enjoys it when it's busy in here."

"Just like you."

Ted shrugged. "I don't mind it. I'm not a hermit or anything. I just prefer to be able to hold a conversation and to hear myself think."

Diego looked around. "So, you're not looking to get into any mischief? You don't plan to stay late and dance with a beautiful stranger?"

Ted laughed. "No."

"When was the last time you even went on a date?"

Ted frowned. "I don't know. It was no doubt whenever you set me up with a friend of one of your conquests. Why?"

Diego laughed. "Because I'm getting worried about you. You don't show any interest in having fun or a good time. You don't show any interest in women anymore."

Ted was about to argue until he realized that his friend might have a point. Then he remembered. "Actually, that's not true."

"It isn't? Who are you interested in?"

"I'm not interested, as such. But just this morning, a woman caught my eye for the first time in a long time." He smiled as he remembered her. "She was beautiful."

Diego dug him in the ribs. "That smile say that there's a story to tell. Who was she? What was she like?"

"It was just a fleeting moment."

Diego sighed. "Those are the best kind."

Ted had to laugh. "You're such a romantic."

"And what's wrong with that? I'm not ashamed of it."

Ted knew he wasn't. It was one of the things he admired about Diego. He was a passionate man. Big and macho, not afraid to voice his opinion about anything—or to laugh, yell or cry. "There's nothing wrong with it."

"I know. So, tell me more about this fleeting moment."

"I was in the gym this morning. Riding the bike and she came and peered through the door. She was …" He smiled. "A beautiful mess. It was only five-thirty, she didn't look like she was even properly awake. Her hair was a mess, no makeup on, wearing a track suit that she might have slept in. But for all of that, she set my heart racing." He wasn't going to tell Diego what other effect she'd had on him. It'd taken a while before he could sit comfortably on the bike again after she left. "She moved like a dancer … her eyes held a kind of sadness … She didn't even see me at first, and she looked embarrassed when she did … I don't know." He shook himself. He hadn't thought about her since.

"We should find her! She must be staying at the hotel."

Ted laughed. "Like I said, it was just a moment. And anyway, I'm sure she'll be leaving tomorrow."

Diego shook his head. "That wouldn't have to matter."

"You're the romantic; I'm the realist, remember?"

"I suppose so."

Chapter Three

Audrey paused before she opened the door to go into the Boathouse. She was looking forward to this evening, she reminded herself. She wasn't going to let Richard being here spoil it for her.

"Are you okay?"

"Thanks, Izzy. I'm fine."

Izzy laughed. "You can say that again. You're looking real fine, girlfriend."

"This thing …" She looked down at the dress. "I think it's magical somehow. It makes me feel great."

"You're the magical one; the dress just reminds you of that. Let's get in there, and you'll see what I mean. Everyone will notice how good you look."

She looked around when they went inside. It was already busy. She recognized a few of Ally and Brayden's friends and smiled and waved to them. Then her daughter appeared out of the crowd.

"Wow, Mom! You look amazing!" Ally wrapped her in a hug.

"Thanks. I think the word you're looking for is fabulous."

Ally laughed. "It is, you're right. Wow! Where did you get that dress? It's gorgeous and it fits like it was—wait, you didn't have it made for you, did you?"

"No! Izzy and I did a little shopping this afternoon."

"You bought that here?"

Izzy smiled. "At Hayes, over at the plaza at Four Mile Creek."

"Oh, wow! I haven't been in there yet. I went in the one in LA once. It's a bit outside my price range."

"You know I don't usually splurge on clothes, but when I tried this on …"

"Absolutely! Whatever you paid for it, it was a bargain."

"Thanks, love. I didn't want to let you down by being your frumpy old mom. Where's your brother? Is he here yet?"

"He's around somewhere." Ally made a face. "Dad collared him to go and say hello to Natalee."

"That's nice."

"Mom! You are such a bad liar! It's not nice at all. I wish they weren't even here. It was Brayden who said we had to invite them—you know what he's like, always trying to be fair and keep the peace."

"And that's how it should be, Ally. He is your father."

"Yeah. And most people wouldn't invite their parents at all. We wanted to invite you because—well, because you're you. I don't see why it means we have to include him. He's definitely not you."

"Thanks. You know I can't comment. Other than to say thank you. It means the world that you guys want me here."

"It wouldn't be the same without you. Oh, no! Why the hell is he bringing them over here?"

Audrey followed her gaze. She'd hoped that by turning up a little later, she'd be able to avoid running into Richard and Natalee. The plan might have worked, too, except Brayden was bringing them over. She loved her son dearly, but sometimes she had to wonder what he was thinking.

"Hey, Mom. Aunt Izzy." He wrapped Audrey in a hug and then pecked Izzy's cheek. "I'm so glad you could all make it. Isn't this great?"

"It's wonderful." Audrey forced herself to smile at Richard and Natalee. "It's nice to see you."

"Thank you." Natalee looked relieved and smiled at her gratefully. She was probably a nice enough person.

"It's good to see you, Audrey." Richard gave her what seemed like a genuine smile. "You look great."

Audrey didn't miss the way Natalee's smile faded when he said that.

"Thanks." She wasn't about to say that he did. He was still handsome, still in great shape, but there was something— maybe it was just the way she saw him that had changed, but there was nothing attractive about him anymore.

"Aren't you going to introduce me?" he asked.

She frowned. "Introduce you? Who to?"

She didn't miss the glint in his eye. "Oh. I'm sorry. I assumed you'd be bringing a date."

"No." If that was his attempt to gloat about the fact that she hadn't found someone new, well, it worked.

Izzy gave him an evil look. "I asked if I could come instead."

"Right." Richard looked pleased with himself.

Audrey was aware that the silence was lengthening to the point of becoming uncomfortable, but she was done with being the fixer of the family. The kids were grown, and Richard was no longer her responsibility.

It was Izzy who broke the silence. "We'll catch you later, kids. We were about to snag a table while we can."

Audrey smiled politely at Richard and Natalee and hugged Ally and Brayden one more time before following Izzy to one of the high-top tables.

"I'm so glad you're rid of him."

Audrey laughed. "I was just thinking the same thing myself."

"You were? That's great. Are you finally there?"

"I've been there for a while now ... you know that."

"I know you've said that, but on the few occasions we've seen him, it didn't seem like you were completely over him."

Audrey thought about it. "If I'm honest, I was over him, but not over the loss of my marriage—of being married, you know? Maybe not even the married part. I just hadn't accepted that I wasn't—that I'm not—loved by someone anymore. Does that make sense?"

"Yeah. It does."

"It's not even that I want or need to be loved by someone. More, that it was a part of my identity for more than thirty years. I was over losing Richard, but I wasn't over losing that part of myself."

"And now you are?"

Audrey looked down at the gorgeous dress Roberto had found for her. It wasn't anything too out of the ordinary. It was a cornflower blue number with a crossover top. It wasn't tight fitting, but it showed off her not-so-slender-anymore figure in a way that made her feel ... sexy. It was strange to say, but it was true. She laughed. "In this dress, I'm happy to say goodbye to that part of myself and figure out who the new me is going to be."

Izzy laughed with her. "That's the spirit. I told you that a new wardrobe can make for a whole new you."

"And you were right. Though, Roberto has to take most of the credit. I see regular trips to LA to shop at Hayes with him in the future."

Izzy raised her glass. "I will happily drink to that. Oh, look. It looks like the band's about to start."

Audrey looked up at the stage where two guys were putting their guitar straps over their heads.

Izzy waggled her eyebrows. "I always wanted to be a groupie."

"Don't even think about it." Audrey smiled to herself when she saw a girl getting up on stage and going to the darker haired guy. She slid her arms up around his neck and pulled his head down for a kiss that left Audrey feeling flustered just watching. She'd just told Izzy that she didn't want or need a man to love her, but watching those two up on the stage made her wonder what it would be like to be loved like that. "My guess is that she's his wife, and she's sending a signal to all the wannabe groupies that he is off limits."

Izzy shrugged. "That's okay. I like the other one better anyway. You really think she's his wife? Would a wife do that?"

Audrey thought about it, and her answer surprised her. She could see where Izzy was coming from. Girlfriends were more passionate and territorial, while wives were more passive—at least in her way of looking at things. But those two on the stage weren't just being passionate; there was love in that kiss, no mistaking it. "I'd put money on it."

"Look at you. You really are coming out of yourself, aren't you? I'll take you up on that bet. You owe me twenty when we discover that they're not married."

Audrey held out her hand to shake on it. Normally, she would have backed down, content to let Izzy be right. But something about tonight—maybe about wearing this dress—made her want to bet on herself.

Izzy watched the girl go back behind the bar. "She's the bartender. It's probably a workplace romance."

"Why don't we go and get ourselves a drink and we can find out?"

"Okay. It looks like we'll be waiting a while to get served if we stay here."

When they got to the bar, the girl greeted them with a smile. "What can I get you ladies?"

"Champagne," said Izzy.

Audrey gave her a puzzled look. "What are we celebrating?"

"The new you!"

"That sounds like something worth celebrating," said the girl behind the bar. "Especially if the new you just bought that dress. Damn, girl!"

Audrey had to laugh. "Thank you. I did. I love it."

"And so you should. Is it champagne, then?"

"Yes, why not. What do you have?"

"I'll bring you the list and then be right back with you. I'm Kenzie by the way."

"Nice to meet you, Kenzie. I'm Audrey, and this is Izzy."

Izzy looked over the wine list. "I think we go should go with a Veuve Clicquot."

Audrey raised an eyebrow. "Are you saying I'm a grand dame?"

"No! I was thinking more along the lines of their marketing slogan—let life surprise you."

"Oh! Yes. I think that fits the bill."

Izzy pulled up a stool. "Shall we sit here until the band takes a break?"

"Why not?" Audrey didn't normally like to sit at the bar, but it seemed that this weekend was a time to break out from her normal. She pulled out a stool and managed to elbow the man sitting beside her.

"I'm sorry."

The man turned and smiled. It was quite a smile, too. He was a very handsome man. Big, muscular, dark hair and dark skin—Latin looking. Handsome as he was, all his smile did for her was remind her of the man in the gym this morning, and the way he'd smiled at her.

"That's okay. No problem," he said and turned back to his companion who Audrey couldn't see, but who she was suddenly convinced was probably some young blonde thing. She shuddered as she turned back to Izzy.

"What's wrong?"

"Nothing. I was just thinking about Richard."

"That explains the look on your face. What are you doing thinking about him?"

"I didn't mean to."

"Good. And I'm sorry. I was trying not to say anything, but the man is an absolute asshole. What he did back there? Pretending that he thought you were here with a date? Total asshole move!"

Audrey shrugged. "Yeah. It was. But—"

"Don't give me any buts; don't make excuses for him."

"I wasn't about to. I was about to say that it doesn't matter to me."

"It matters to me. I wish I could find you some gorgeous guy that you could flaunt in front of him. That'd wipe the smile off his face."

Audrey chuckled. "I appreciate you being so protective of me, but I doubt he'd care anyway."

"Oh, he'd care all right. His eyes nearly popped out of his head when he saw you in that dress."

"Why would he notice his ex-wife when he's now married to the young and lovely Natalee? She's so pretty."

"She might be pretty, but like I told you, you, my friend, are beautiful. She's a girl; you're a woman."

"Thanks."

~ ~ ~

Diego turned to say something to the woman who'd just sat down beside him, and Ted prepared himself for the flirting

that was no doubt about to commence. To his surprise, it
didn't. Instead, Diego turned back and jerked his head,
indicating that Ted should take a look for himself. He waited a
few moments and then tried, but he couldn't see anything
other than the back of her head. Her shoulder length brown
hair was nice, but other than that … He turned to look in the
mirror behind the bar, and his heart thudded to a halt when he
saw her. It was *her!* The woman from the gym this morning.
He'd known then that her track suit didn't do her justice, but
he'd had no idea just how beautiful she'd look when she was
dressed up.

Diego smirked at him and mouthed *Wow!*

Ted shook his head rapidly. He couldn't let Diego go getting
any ideas. She was his! He bit down on his bottom lip and told
himself to reel it in. She was hardly his. But he couldn't let his
opportunity go by, and there was no way he could let Diego
take it from him.

"What?"

Ted struggled to keep his voice down and yet still be heard
over the band. "That's *her.*"

"Her who? Oh!" Diego grinned. "Your friend from the gym?
Your beautiful mess?"

Ted nodded.

"So, what are you waiting for?" Diego began to turn around,
but Ted caught his arm.

His heart was still racing; he needed a moment to compose
himself—to figure out what to say. "Give me a minute."

"If you say so."

They both stayed quiet, and Ted strained to catch her
conversation with her friend. After a few moments, Diego
raised an eyebrow at him. He was eavesdropping, too.

"Did you hear that? I think you should make her friend's wish come true. She's seeking a gorgeous man that your beautiful mess can flaunt in front of her ex-husband. Can I tell her that she's found one?"

Ted shook his head. That really wasn't his style. He'd bide his time, find a moment to introduce himself properly. He watched as both women fell silent and listened to the band.

When the song ended, the friend waggled her eyebrows. "Come on Audrey, you can't tell me you'd turn the drummer down if he asked you? He's hot!"

Audrey. He liked the name. He turned to watch her face in the mirror, expecting to hear her say that yes, she found Eddie as hot as her friend did.

What he heard instead made his heart feel as though it might beat out of his ribcage.

"Obviously, I can see the appeal. But you know younger guys don't do it for me."

Ted let out the breath he didn't realize he'd been holding.

He smiled when he saw her chuckle. "You know me, Izzy. That guy is your type. I, on the other hand, wish I could meet his father."

Diego spun around to look at him with a big grin on his face. "Sorry, mi amigo, but I must." He turned back toward the women, put his hand on Audrey's shoulder and said, "Wish granted."

Ted watched the confusion on her face. She probably thought Diego was making a move on her, and there was no way he could ever be taken for Eddie's father. She gave him a puzzled smile and he leaned back in his seat so that she could see past him to Ted.

Her gaze locked with his, and his heart clenched in his chest. She took his breath away; she was just that beautiful.

He got down from his seat and went to shake her hand. "It's a pleasure to see you again. I'm Ted." He jerked his head toward the stage. "And that's my son, Eddie."

Chapter Four

Audrey felt as though time stood still. She was staring into his eyes and she couldn't look away. They were such kind eyes. His hand was still wrapped around hers. She knew she should say something. She cleared her throat. "It's nice to see you again."

He looked as though he was expecting her to say more. What did he want? To hear just how thrilled she was to see him again? That he looked even sexier tonight than he had in the gym this morning? Did he want to know that the warmth from his hand—which still hadn't let go of hers—was spreading all through her, touching parts of her that hadn't felt any heat in way too long?

Izzy kicked her foot, startling her back to her senses. "I'm Audrey, and this is Izzy."

Izzy grinned and leaned forward to shake first Diego's hand and then Ted's. "How do you two know each other?"

Ted turned his head toward her, but his eyes never left Audrey's as he replied. "We met briefly this morning."

"Oh! You're the guy from the gym!"

Audrey's heart raced. Trust Izzy! Now he'd know that she'd talked about him after seeing him this morning.

His smile said he didn't mind. In fact, he seemed quite pleased. His friend confirmed that impression.

He held his hand out to shake with Izzy and nodded at Audrey. "I heard about this brief meeting, too." He gave Izzy a conspiratorial smile. "I'm Diego, by the way. Since Ted seems to have forgotten to introduce me. Can we buy you a drink, ladies?"

Ted raised an eyebrow at Audrey, and it sent shivers chasing each other down her spine. Her wayward imagination got the impression that he was inquiring about more than buying her a drink.

Izzy waved the bottle of champagne. "We're fine for drinks, thanks. But we'd love for you to join us."

"Another bottle, then." Diego grinned. "And tell us what you're celebrating, so we can join in?"

"It's my—" began Audrey.

"Audrey here is beginning a new chapter," Izzy spoke over her.

Diego waved Kenzie over to order more champagne.

"What kind of chapter?" asked Ted.

She felt as though his voice vibrated through her—and it felt good. She smiled, feeling a little embarrassed. She could hardly explain. She was celebrating the fact that she finally felt like her own person again.

Izzy didn't mind answering the question for her. "Audrey's had a tough time for the last few years, and now she's coming into her own." She raised her glass and smiled at them. "She's ready to have some fun."

Audrey didn't know where to look. Izzy couldn't make it more obvious that she was implying that the door was open for Ted to … to what? To talk to her? To dance with her? To take her home?

His smile was so kind. It seemed that he sensed her discomfort and wanted to put her at ease. "I'm glad your hard times are behind you. I hope this next chapter is the best one yet."

For a crazy moment, she believed that he was including himself in that chapter, that he was saying ... no! She had to pull herself together. He was just being kind and helping to get her out of the spot that Izzy—she'd throttle her later!—had put her in.

"Thank you."

Diego held up a fresh bottle of champagne and two more glasses. "May I suggest that we move to a table? The band is about to take their break, and that will mean a rush at the bar."

Izzy slid down from her stool with a grin. "I was just thinking the same thing. There's a booth open over there, see?"

Ted smiled at Audrey as the others headed toward the booth. "Is this okay with you? Diego can be a little ... full-on."

She had to chuckle. "You may have noticed that Izzy's the same way."

"Do you mind?"

She shook her head. She didn't mind at all that their friends were giving them this opportunity. "Do you?"

"The only part I mind is that they're joining us. I wish I'd seen you first, and that we could take a table by ourselves."

Audrey's heart hammered in her chest, and at the same time, butterflies took to flight in her stomach.

"Was that too forward of me?" he asked when she didn't say anything.

"No. It's not that."

He raised an eyebrow.

What the heck? She was just going to say it. "Honestly, I was thinking the same thing."

His smile was back. "Do you want to leave them to drink champagne? We could get out of here. Get a drink and talk somewhere quieter."

She shook her head sadly. "That sounds like just the kind of thing the old me would never do, and yet the new me would love to."

"Isn't this a new chapter? Don't let the old you win."

She sighed. "I can't. This is my children's birthday party. I can't just leave."

"Ah. Okay. I'm sorry."

He looked disappointed, and she wanted him to know that she was, too. "It's not a brush off. I just can't walk out on my children's party."

"No. I understand. Maybe …" He stopped. "We should catch up with them." He nodded to where Izzy and Diego had claimed the empty booth.

Audrey wanted to ask what his maybe had been. She wanted to suggest that they could do something tomorrow instead. But tomorrow was Sunday, and he'd no doubt be leaving to go back to his life, wherever that was. She glanced at his left hand and was relieved to see that there was no wedding band. Though that didn't necessarily mean anything.

~ ~ ~

Ted slid into the booth to sit beside Diego who slid a glass of champagne in front of him. "Let's toast to a new chapter."

Ted caught Audrey's gaze. He couldn't keep his eyes off her, and it seemed that she felt the same way. It made his heart race. "To new beginnings," he said and raised his glass toward her.

She raised hers with a smile. "New beginnings," she echoed.

"So," Izzy grinned around at them, "we know that Eddie is your son, and Diego tells me that you guys live in Laguna Beach. What else do we need to know about you?"

Ted laughed. Izzy struck him as a female version of Diego. "What do you want to know?" he asked.

"Everything." She looked more serious as she continued. "I suppose the first important thing to get out of the way is, where's Eddie's mom?"

She might as well have thrown a drink in his face. The question brought him down to earth with a bump. He didn't talk about Irene.

Diego caught his eye. He knew the score.

Audrey was watching him carefully. He knew what she must be thinking, but it couldn't be further from the truth.

"Where is she? I have no idea. I haven't seen or heard from her in …" he had to think about it, "almost twenty-five years."

Izzy looked thrilled to hear it. Although she hadn't picked up on how uncomfortable the question had made him, it seemed that Audrey had. She gave him an apologetic smile, and he'd swear that there was understanding in her eyes.

"What about you, Audrey?" asked Diego.

Dammit. It was typical Diego, stepping up to defend him. He didn't need it. And it wasn't as though they didn't already know her situation—from their eavesdropping. Her ex-husband was here, with his new, young wife. Ted turned to glare at his friend. He shouldn't have put her on the spot like that.

"I've been divorced for almost three years now. Unfortunately, I can't say I haven't seen him in that time. In fact, he's here this evening. This is our children's birthday party."

"And what about you, Diego?" Ted didn't see why he should get away with it. He knew full well that Diego and Izzy were trying to play matchmaker and protective friend at the same time, since his attraction to Audrey was so obvious. But since they were both behaving badly, as far as he was concerned, he wanted them to be put on the spot, too.

Diego shrugged. Nothing phased him. He smiled at Audrey. "My son is here, also. His name is Zack. His mother left us when he was six."

"I'm sorry." Audrey's expression said a lot about her. It told Ted that she truly was sorry to hear that—and also that she couldn't imagine a mother ever leaving her child.

"And before anyone asks me to share my tale of woe," said Izzy. "I have no children. I couldn't, and I've been divorced for eight years from a man who swore to me that it didn't matter. He's remarried with a six-year-old daughter." Her smile didn't fade as she spoke, but Ted could only guess at the pain behind it.

"Well." Audrey looked around the table. "Now that we've got that out of the way ..." she smiled. "Perhaps we can bring it back to regular chitchat. Are you two here for the weekend? Where's home?"

Ted liked her for wanting to move the conversation past that awkward moment. "Home is Laguna Beach. And I'm here for the week." He smiled. "My grandson asked me to stay."

Diego cocked his head to one side. "Did I know this?"

Ted laughed. "I thought I told you, but perhaps I forgot."

Diego shrugged and looked at Izzy. "I'm going home to Laguna tomorrow. You?"

She grinned. "I have to go home tomorrow, too." She turned to Audrey. "But this one is staying until next weekend, while I go back and run the office."

Audrey laughed. "Don't go for the sympathy vote. You're the one who insisted I take some time off. I can come back with you, if you like."

Izzy shook her head rapidly. "No way!"

Ted couldn't believe his luck. He'd assumed that they would be leaving tomorrow. Instead, Audrey was staying the whole week—and her friend wasn't. "What are you plans while you're here?"

She smiled at him. "To rest and relax."

"To have some fun," added Izzy. She caught Ted's gaze and gave him the hint of a nod.

"Perhaps you can both have some fun," said Diego.

Ted wanted to tell them both to butt out. Audrey looked as though she felt the same way.

"Would you excuse me for a moment?" she asked. "The kids are coming over."

Ted turned to see a young man and woman coming toward them. As he watched, Eddie stepped out of the crowd, and they stopped to chat with him. For some reason, it made him happy to think that they all knew each other.

He glanced back at Audrey and she smiled. "They did mention that they knew the guys in the band."

He got up. "Do you want to go and say hello?" He was glad when she got to her feet and joined him. He knew that Diego and Izzy were only trying to help them along, but he'd much prefer to do without their help.

"Mom! There you are." The girl came toward them. "We were looking for you. How do you know Eddie's dad?"

Audrey cast a shy glance at him, and he guessed that she wouldn't want to explain that they'd just met.

"We have some mutual friends," he explained. It wasn't a lie; he now knew Izzy and she knew Diego.

Eddie stepped forward. "I hope you're all having a good time?"

"It's great, thanks." Ted smiled at his son and then looked at Audrey as he added. "Much better than I expected."

"I'm surprised you're still here. I thought you were going to duck out when it got busy."

Ted gave Audrey a rueful smile. "So did I, but I changed my mind." He hoped that she would understand that she was the one who'd changed it. "I'm sorry," he added. "I haven't introduced you. Audrey, this is my son, Eddie."

"Nice to meet you."

"You, too. Ally and Brayden have told me so much about you. I'm glad you could come."

Ted made a mental note to ask Eddie what he knew about her.

"Thanks. I'm honored to be here." Ted loved the way she smiled at her kids. "Ally and Brayden, this is Ted."

They greeted him warmly. Ally especially seemed pleased to meet him.

"Well, I hate to break it up," said Eddie, "but I'm going to have to get back on stage soon."

Brayden looked around. "Do you have a minute? I said I'd introduce you to my dad."

Both Audrey and Ally tensed at that. "We can find him later," Ally said.

"No, look. There he is." Brayden waved at a man who looked to be around Ted's age who was standing with a woman who looked to be more Ally and Brayden's age. He guessed that was the ex and his new wife.

Ally scowled and gave her mom an apologetic look.

Audrey shrugged and mouthed *It's okay.*

Ted felt as though he should probably go and sit back down, but he didn't want to. Instead, he watched them approach. The wife was pretty. Izzy had been right, though; the wife was just a girl, while Audrey was a woman—a very beautiful woman.

He watched as Brayden introduced Eddie to Richard and Natalee. He could tell that Eddie took an instant dislike to

Richard. He had great instincts about people. He doubted that anyone else would pick up on it, but Ted could tell that Eddie didn't like the guy.

Eddie turned to him with a smile. "This is my dad, Ted Rawlins."

Richard's eyes widened. "As in Ted Rawlins of Rawlins-Águila?"

Ted nodded. It shouldn't be a surprise that Richard recognized his name. He could feel Audrey's eyes on him. He'd guess that she wasn't familiar with it.

Richard grinned and stepped forward eagerly to shake his hand. "It's a pleasure. I hope we'll get the chance to talk some more. In fact, do you want to come and—"

Ted couldn't manage to keep his smile in place. He could sense just what kind of guy Richard was. He encountered them all the time. The ones who had no time for anyone who couldn't help them advance in some way, and who were all over those who they thought could be of use to them. "No. I don't mix business and pleasure." He turned to Audrey and without stopping to question whether he should, he put his hand in the small of her back and drew her a little closer. "And tonight's about pleasure."

The expression on Richard's face told him that he'd made the right move. He was stunned. It was obvious. And he was not happy. To his relief, Audrey seemed very happy. She leaned a little closer to him and gave him a grateful smile.

"Oh. Of course." Richard recovered quickly. "Some other time." He backed away a few steps and then seemed to remember his wife. He put an arm around her shoulders and nodded at the group before steering her away.

Eddie gave Ted a puzzled look. "Dare I ask?"

"Probably best not."

"No way!" exclaimed Ally. "Are you guys a thing? Or were you just helping mom out? Either way …" She held her hand up in the air and Ted only missed a couple of beats before he high-fived her. She grinned. "You are one of my new favorite people."

Brayden was looking at them and Ted remembered that he still had his hand on Audrey's back. If her son didn't like it, he should probably stop, but he didn't want to.

Brayden smiled. "*Are* you guys a thing, then?"

Ted looked down at Audrey and was thrilled when she smiled. She didn't deny it, didn't explain that they'd never laid eyes on each other before this morning. Her smile made his heart race.

He decided his best bet was to follow her lead. He smiled at their kids and shrugged.

Eddie chuckled. "Does that mean you're not answering yet?"

He nodded.

"Well, I'm saying that you are." Ally grinned. "Especially to Dad."

"How does he know you?" asked Brayden.

Ted pursed his lips. He could honestly claim that he didn't know. But the honest answer was that most people who were in any kind of business in Southern California knew of Rawlins-Águila Bank, even if they didn't know him personally.

"He's a banker," explained Eddie.

"Looks like Chase wants you back up there, Eddie," said Ally.

"I'd better go." Eddie grinned at Ted. "I'll call you tomorrow."

"Sure."

"It was great to meet you, Audrey. I hope I'll see you again."

~ ~ ~

Audrey tried to get her heart back under control as she watched Eddie make his way back onto the stage. It was a difficult task, though. Ted's hand still rested in the small of her back. Waves of heat emanated out from where it touched. Shivers chased each other down her spine and she didn't dare look, but she guessed that all the little hairs on her arms were standing on end.

Ally turned back to her and gave her a meaningful look. "I know you weren't planning to stay all night. We don't mind if you want to duck out whenever you're ready. Do we, Brayden?"

It made Audrey smile that even her son picked up on what she meant. "Yeah. Err, I mean no. You take off whenever you want. We're just glad you came."

"It was nice to meet you." Ally smiled at Ted.

"Yeah," agreed Brayden. "We'll see you soon, I guess."

Audrey held her breath wondering what Ted would say.

"I hope so."

Once they'd gone, she turned to look up into his eyes. "Thank you."

He nodded. "I overheard you talking with Izzy earlier. She was right. He's a fool. Natalee is pretty. But you ..." He looked into her eyes. "You're a beautiful woman, Audrey."

She heard herself sigh and felt as though her knees might give way underneath her.

He smiled. "Do you want to stay and show him what a fool he is?"

"What? How do you mean?"

"Most men are idiots when it comes to women. They only understand a woman's worth when they see her with someone else."

For a moment, Audrey wondered what had happened in his life to make him say that. But she was more focused on what he meant about her.

"He let you go. Seeing you with me makes him realize what a huge mistake that was. I guarantee you that he's kicking himself right now, feeling like a fool."

She smiled. "In that case, I wouldn't mind staying for a little while. If you don't mind pretending."

Her breath caught in her chest as he smiled down at her. "I'm not pretending, Audrey. I'm hoping."

Chapter Five

Audrey didn't miss the glint in Diego's eye when she and Ted sat back down. She got the feeling that he was just like Izzy.

Izzy grinned at her. "I see you had the chance to talk with Richard?"

She nodded. She knew what her friend was getting at—that her wish for a gorgeous man to flaunt in front of Richard had been granted.

Diego grinned at Ted. "Judging by the way he was so eager to meet you, I'd guess that he knew who you are?"

Ted smiled back at him. "He did."

Audrey turned to look at him. "It seems he's more in the know than I am."

"He's probably heard mention of me in business circles."

Diego chuckled. "My friend is too modest. I, on the other hand, am not. We're bankers. Rawlins-Águila is a well-known and respected private bank."

Izzy raised her eyebrows. "So, Ted Rawlins and Diego Águila?"

"That's right."

"And what about you ladies," asked Ted. "What do you do?"

"Advertising," said Audrey.

"Do you work for anyone we might know?" asked Diego.

Izzy laughed. "We both work for someone you know: Audrey."

Audrey was used to men assuming that she was someone's assistant.

"You have your own agency?" asked Ted. "Where are you based?"

"The office is in Ventura. We're just a small team."

Izzy rolled her eyes and looked at Diego. "My friend is as bad as yours for being overly modest. She went out on her own after her divorce from *him*. You know what the name Richard usually gets shortened to, don't you? Well, in his case, there couldn't be a more appropriate nick-name."

"Izzy!" Audrey made a face at her. She agreed with the sentiment but didn't think that her friend should go sharing it with people who they'd just met.

Diego looked puzzled for a moment, then laughed when he figured out what Izzy meant. There was such kindness in Ted's smile when he looked at Audrey. He didn't feel like someone she'd just met. He felt like a friend—a good friend—who understood.

"Anyway," Izzy continued. "The two of them were in business together. Audrey did all the work. But the advertising world is still like an old boys' club. So, when they separated, most of the business stayed with Richard. He's pretty much run the agency into the ground now, from what I hear."

"That's not true," said Audrey. She didn't feel any need to defend Richard, but she didn't want her friend to run him down, either.

Izzy held up a hand. "Okay. Sorry. I'll stop." She smiled at Ted and Diego. "The short version of the story is that Audrey went out on her own after the divorce and now runs a digital advertising agency that has won numerous awards in the last couple of years."

Ted caught Audrey's eye. "What kind of clients do you work with?"

Diego chuckled. "I think he's wondering whether you work with banks."

Audrey smiled. "We work with anyone who's looking to increase their reach online. But I'm here to take a break from work. So, if you don't mind, can we move the conversation along?"

"Why don't we move it onto the dance floor?" suggested Diego.

Izzy was on her feet before Audrey had the chance to wonder if she wanted to dance with Ted at her kids' birthday bash.

Ted got to his feet, but he let Diego and Izzy go ahead of him before turning to Audrey. "Do you want to dance, or would you rather stay here?"

He was such a handsome man. Her heart fluttered in her chest when he raised an eyebrow at her.

"It's not that I don't want to dance with you …" she began.

He nodded, and she was thrilled to see disappointment in his eyes. "I understand. Your children. Your ex-husband …"

Audrey glanced over at Diego and Izzy who were already making their way onto the dance floor. It was crowded, but Izzy elbowed a space for herself. The girl she hustled out of her way looked familiar. Oh, it was Natalee. And Richard was up there dancing with her. He'd always refused to dance with Audrey. She felt a little stab of resentment in her chest. She'd spent all those years taking care of their children and of him, while he'd refused to indulge her in so many of the things she enjoyed. She looked back at Ted.

He'd followed her gaze and no doubt seen the same thing she had. "Are you sure you don't want to?"

"No, I'm not sure at all."

He offered her his hand. "I promise I'll be a gentleman, but I get the feeling that it's far too long since you danced."

She nodded, not knowing what she could say to explain, and at the same time feeling as though she didn't even need to. Somehow, he understood. She took hold of his hand and let him lead her toward the dance floor.

Just before they reached it, he stopped and leaned in to speak closer to her ear. She had to focus hard to catch his words, not because of the music but because of the shivers racing down her neck and spine.

"Richard is already watching you like a hawk. Do you want him to see you dancing with a friend, or …"

She turned her head to look at him. He was so close, their noses almost touched. He smelled so good. She closed her eyes and breathed in, then came to her senses and looked into his eyes. She didn't know what to say, but she could tell that Ted knew. He knew that she wanted Richard to see her enjoying herself with a handsome man—that she wanted to feel attractive and desirable.

She smiled. "It's probably petty of me, but I prefer the *or …* option."

"It's not petty, if you ask me. If a man is crazy enough to let a woman like you go, he should be reminded of what a fool he is." He smiled. "Not that you asked me. And perhaps I'm only rationalizing my desire to be the one who gets to remind him."

Audrey's breath caught in her chest. "You don't mind doing that for me?"

He squeezed her hand. "I don't mind, and you need to understand, I'm doing it for me, too."

~ ~ ~

Ted had to force himself to step away and lead her out onto the dance floor when all he really wanted to do was close the last few inches between their lips and kiss her. He drew in a deep breath. Maybe he'd kiss her before the night was over. He knew he wanted to, and he'd guess that she did, too. But not here, not surrounded by so many people. Especially not in front of her ex and her kids and Eddie.

Just as they made themselves some space near Diego and Izzy, who were having a fine old time by the looks of them, the song came to an end. Ted hoped that whatever Eddie played next wouldn't be anything too wild. He wasn't the best dancer and while that hadn't seemed important compared to his desire to dance with Audrey, it seemed a lot more so now he was here.

He glanced up at his son when he heard the first few bars of an old ballad. He hadn't heard Eddie and Chase play it before, and he got the feeling that it was for his benefit. The lyrics spoke of friends and lovers and the people who never left your heart. He looked back at Audrey who swayed to the music. She looked uncomfortable, and he immediately understood why. Couples were moving together all around them—even Diego and Izzy held each other.

He smiled and held both hands out to her. He wanted to close his arms around her, but he wanted it to be her decision. He was thrilled when she came closer and slid one arm up around his neck, resting her other hand on his chest. He held her against him and looked down into her eyes.

There was laughter in them as she smiled up at him. "I didn't know they were going to start playing the slow ones."

"Neither did I. He tightened his arm around her waist and held her a little closer, loving the feel of her against his chest. "I'll be sure to thank Eddie later, though."

Her eyes widened and she glanced up at his son before looking back at him. "You think he did it on purpose?"

He shrugged. "I've never heard them play this one on stage before, and it's one of my favorite songs."

"Mine, too."

For some reason that made him happy. He didn't know her at all yet, but he liked everything that he'd seen and heard so far. And he wanted to get to know her; he knew that much. "I know I should probably wait until the end of the evening before I ask this, but ... since you're here for the rest of the week and I am, too, can I see you again?"

Her smile answered before her lips moved. "Yes. I'd like that."

"Thank you."

His gaze locked with hers. Her eyes were a beautiful bluey-green, like the ocean under a sunny sky. He could get lost in them if he wasn't careful. And he needed to be careful, he realized as he found himself leaning closer. Kissing her felt like the most natural next move, but he had to hold himself back. Her eyelids drooped, and he knew she was as lost in the feeling as he was. He rested his forehead against hers and her eyes flew open.

"Do you have any idea how hard it is for me not to kiss you right now?" he asked.

For a moment, his heart sank, and he felt like a fool when she laughed. Had he read it wrong?

Her laughter faded away and she brought her hand up to touch his cheek, sending electric currents racing through him. "I'm sorry. I was laughing at myself, not at you. When you asked if I know how hard it is ..." She dropped her gaze, but a smile still played on her lips. "Honestly, that's exactly what I was trying not to focus on."

He had to laugh. "Ah! Sorry."

She pressed herself a little closer against him and made it even harder. "Don't apologize! I'm taking it as a compliment. I'm shocked at myself for mentioning it, but ..." She looked up into his eyes. "I feel safe to say it with you."

His heart clenched in his chest. "You are." Were the only words he could manage.

If his urge to kiss her had been strong before, it was almost overwhelming now. He could feel his head lowering, and there was nothing he could do to stop it. Not until someone jostled them from the side, and he had to brace himself to keep Audrey upright.

He scowled at the idiot who'd just crashed into them, then pressed his lips together when he realized who it was.

"Oh, gosh. I'm so sorry," said Natalee.

Richard glowered at him but didn't speak.

"That's okay," said Audrey. "We should do a better job of keeping our distance." She tightened her hold on Ted as she danced away from them.

"Sorry about that," she said once they were over the other side of the dance floor.

Ted smiled. "It was hardly your fault. He's rattled, isn't he?"

She nodded. "I'm surprised, but yes he is. I shouldn't be though. It must be a surprise to him to see me with you. He hasn't thought of me as a woman in years."

Ted shook his head. "Then he's an idiot. And his loss is my gain." He stopped abruptly. That was too much to even think, let alone say, at this point. But it was how he felt, and he didn't see any point in hiding it. He gave her a rueful smile. "Sorry. You have my head turned right around. I should be going more cautiously, shouldn't I?"

Her eyes shone as she looked up at him. "Maybe. I don't remember how these things are even supposed to work. But I'm glad you're not being cautious. I don't want to be."

He shifted his hips away from her a little. Her words made him wonder what kind of cautious she was talking about. He didn't want to rush into anything, but he couldn't deny that it was getting harder.

~ ~ ~

"Are you guys okay? I can't believe Richard. I told you he's a Dick!"

Izzy and Diego had appeared by their side, or maybe Audrey had danced Ted in their direction. She wasn't sure quite what had just happened—other than the fact that Richard had jostled them, and Ted had said that Richard's loss was his gain. She was trying hard to process what exactly he might mean by that, but she was failing. All she could focus on was the way he made her feel—and how wonderful he was.

Izzy stared into her eyes. "Are you okay?"

She nodded. "I'm fine. It was nothing."

Diego scowled. "I wouldn't call that nothing."

"It's okay." Ted reassured him. "He's hardly a problem. I almost feel sorry for him."

Diego and Izzy both looked at him, and he laughed. "Come on. It's obvious that he's just realized what he's lost." He smiled at Audrey. "He's jealous."

Izzy laughed. "Of course, he is. But there's no need for him to behave like a spoiled child. That was ridiculous the way he ran into you like that."

Audrey shrugged. "It doesn't matter. No harm done." She wanted to get back to dancing with Ted, back to their conversation and where it might go. She didn't want to waste this precious time where she got to feel his arms around her and to move their bodies to the music. She felt heat in her cheeks and was grateful that none of them could hear her thoughts.

The song came to an end and she was disappointed to hear the next one was much more upbeat. Ted gave her a rueful smile. "Is it time to sit back down?"

"Probably." She wasn't the best dancer and trying to shake her butt to the music held much less appeal than shuffling and swaying with him.

Izzy caught her arm. "We'll be back," she told Ted.

Audrey frowned as her friend dragged her toward the ladies' room. "Where are we going?"

"To do the traditional girly chat in the bathroom," Izzy told her with a laugh. "I need to know what you're thinking. Do you like him? Do you want to leave now? Do you want me to leave separately so that you and Ted can do your own thing, or do you want me to rescue you?"

Audrey laughed as she pushed her way through the door into the ladies' room. "What do you think?"

"I think you should take off with him, just the two of you. Catch a cab back to the lodge, go for a romantic walk on the beach and then take him back to your room and bonk his brains out!"

"Izzy!"

"What?! You asked me what I think. I told you. And if you don't do that, then I think you're nuts."

Audrey swallowed. She wanted to say that she would never dream of doing something like that, and before tonight that would have been the truth, but right now she couldn't help but wonder … what if …? No!

Izzy was watching her closely. "Oh, my God! You're thinking about it, aren't you?"

Audrey shook her head rapidly.

"You're blushing and everything!"

"Okay! I admit. It's tempting. He's ... he's so ..."

"Hot!" Izzy nodded her agreement.

"No! Well, yes, he is, but not that ... at least, not just that," she added hurriedly. "He's so kind and understanding, I feel like he just knows what I'm thinking."

Izzy rolled her eyes. "He probably does. He knows that you're thinking that you wouldn't mind taking him back to your room."

"No. It's not like that."

"Oh, Audrey."

"Seriously. Just because you think it's okay to go out and hook up, you think everyone else is the same. He's not like that."

"Maybe." Izzy blew out a sigh. "I just want you to have some fun, that's all. He seems like a nice guy. But I don't want you to go getting your hopes up that he's something special while he's just thinking that you'd be a nice way to spend the night."

"He already asked if he can see me again."

"Okay, maybe he's thinking you might be a nice way to spend the week."

"And what would be wrong with that? I thought you'd approve."

Izzy touched her arm. "I would. You know all I want is to see you have some fun and be happy. I just don't want you to go hoping for something more."

Audrey opened her mouth but though better of it. She was about to ask why she shouldn't hope for more. Ted was an attractive man. He'd made no secret that he was interested in her. Maybe Izzy was right, and he was only interested in sex. Would that be such a bad thing?

"Go on," said Izzy. "Spit it out, whatever you were about to say."

Audrey smiled. "I was about to prove you right by saying that there might be something more between us. It feels like there could be. But even if there isn't, that's fine too." She waggled her eyebrows. "Maybe you've taught me well, and maybe I only want to use him for his body!"

Izzy laughed. "Nice try, but we both know that's not who you are. I say have some fun with him, enjoy it, let yourself be a little wild, but don't go getting invested. I don't want to see you get hurt."

"Thanks."

"So, do you want to stay a while longer. Do you want us all to leave together, or are you feeling brave?"

Audrey thought about it. "I'm feeling brave, but maybe we should stay a while longer?"

"The kids already told you they don't mind if you go."

"I know, but ..."

"But nothing. Come on. Let's go. I can keep Diego here, and you two can go get a cab."

"And what will you and Diego be doing later?"

Izzy pursed her lips. "Not a damned thing."

"Don't tell me you don't like him?"

Izzy rolled her eyes. "I'm not a liar. He's gorgeous! But he's all big macho man, and you know I can't cope with guys like that."

Audrey smirked. "Of course, you prefer younger guys you can boss around."

"It's not about bossing them around, it's ..." Izzy laughed. "Okay, maybe it is. I just can't handle big macho men."

"Diego seems sweet, though."

"He is, but we're not a good match. We're cut from the same cloth. We're both used to being the alpha."

"Why does that matter if you're both going home together?"

Izzy shrugged. "It doesn't. Anyway, enough deflecting attention away from you and Ted. Let's get back out there and get you two on your way."

"I need to say goodnight to the kids."

"Okay, we'll find them on the way out."

Chapter Six

Diego grinned at Ted. "You seem smitten."

He couldn't hide his smile. "I am."

Diego grasped his shoulder. "Do you want me to make myself scarce? I believe Izzy will be a willing accomplice in leaving the two of you alone."

"No. Thanks, but ... no."

Diego gave him a puzzled look. "You don't expect me to believe that you don't want to get the lovely Audrey all to yourself?"

"I wouldn't lie to you. But I don't think she'd be comfortable with it." He smiled. "Though if what you're really saying is that you want to disappear with Izzy ..."

Diego laughed. "I'd love to, but alas. She's not interested."

"I don't believe that for a moment. I saw you dancing together. And besides, I thought the great Diego Águila could persuade any woman."

Diego swaggered his shoulders. "I like to think so, but part of that is knowing who wants to be persuaded, and Izzy doesn't. She's a beautiful woman; she knows what she wants and she knows how to have a good time. I'm not her idea of a good time."

Ted was genuinely puzzled. "I don't get it."

Diego chuckled. "Of course, you don't. You're not someone who plays the game. I am, so is Izzy. She likes her men younger and more ... submissive."

Ted raised an eyebrow.

He laughed. "Not the in the full-on dominatrix style—I don't think—but she likes to be the boss."

"Ah, I get it. You two both like to be the star of the show?"

"Something like that. I could make an exception for her— she's quite something, but you heard her, she was drooling over your son."

Ted laughed. "And your ego can't handle that?"

Diego shrugged. "The point is tonight is about you and Audrey. What do you want; do you want us all to share a cab home?"

"I think that'd be best. She's here all week, and so am I. There's no rush."

Diego shook his head. "Whatever you say, my friend."

Ted got to his feet when Audrey and Izzy came back to the table.

"More champagne?" suggested Diego.

"No, thanks," said Izzy. "We were thinking we should get going."

Ted's heart sank. Perhaps the question wasn't whether he and Audrey should leave without Diego and Izzy, but rather whether Audrey wanted to leave with him at all. He caught her gaze and was relieved when she smiled.

"We thought maybe we should take a cab back to the lodge now. I imagine there'll be a long line to get one after the band finishes." She hesitated and Ted would swear that he saw Izzy kick her foot. "Since we're all staying over there ... we could share a cab and have a drink at the bar when we get back ... if you'd like?"

Ted was thrilled that she asked. He didn't get the chance to reply before Diego answered for him. "Absolutely. We should go." He got to his feet with a grin.

Audrey gave Ted a shy smile. "I didn't mean right this minute. I need to say goodbye to Ally and Brayden first."

"Can we come and wish them a happy birthday?"

"Of course."

As they made their way through the crowded bar, Ted spotted Richard watching them. He caught Ted's gaze and visibly tried to turn his frown into a polite smile. It didn't quite work.

Ted already despised the man. The way he'd fawned over him when he realized who he was made Ted's skin crawl. He'd known too many men like that—men who valued money and influence over anything else. He gave him a curt nod and couldn't help putting his hand in the small of Audrey's back as they found her daughter, Ally.

Ally kissed Audrey's cheek and smiled at Ted. "Thanks for coming, Mom. It was lovely to meet you, Ted. I hope we'll see you again soon."

"I do, too. And happy birthday, to you."

"Thanks. I don't know where Brayden got to, but don't worry about him, Mom. You guys get going."

Audrey looked around. "I'd like to say goodnight to him."

"You'll see him tomorrow."

Ted got the impression that Ally wanted her mom to go. He understood why when he saw Brayden coming toward them, with Richard and his wife in tow.

Ally blew out a sigh. "I tried."

"It's okay," said Audrey. "We can be civil."

"I know you two can; I mean him! I saw what he did when you were all dancing."

"It's fine," said Audrey. "Leave it. I just want to say goodnight to Brayden, and then we'll go."

Ted watched her hug her son. It was obvious how much she loved her children—and how much they loved her.

"We're leaving now. Thanks again for having us here."

"Thanks for coming, Mom." Brayden turned to Izzy and hugged her. "Thanks, Aunt Izzy." He stood back and looked at Diego, apparently wondering whether this was someone whose name he should remember.

Diego smiled. "Thanks for having us."

"I don't believe we've been introduced," Richard said to Diego.

Ted had to hide a smile as Diego put his arm around Izzy and she played right up to it, leaning against him with a smile as he extended his hand. "Diego Águila. And you must be Richard?"

Richard nodded.

"And these are your children?" Diego continued. "Ally and Brayden, the birthday twins and …" He stared at Natalee and frowned. "Your younger daughter?"

Ted had to bite back a laugh at the way Richard scowled, and Audrey and Izzy tried not to laugh.

"Actually, this is my wife, Natalee."

Diego took her hand and kissed the back of it with more bravado than Ted would ever be able to muster. "Forgive me."

Natalee's cheeks flushed as she nodded and gawked. It was obvious that she was bowled over.

Richard took her other hand and pulled her away. "Come on, we're leaving."

Diego tried to look apologetic after they'd gone. "Did I do something wrong?" he asked innocently.

Izzy slapped his arm with a laugh. "You did wonderfully—and you know it."

Ted had to wonder by the way Diego grinned whether he was really as indifferent to Izzy as he'd made out.

Audrey chuckled. "I should feel bad, but I don't."

Ted pressed his hand into the small of her back. "I get the impression that he made you feel bad for far too many years."

She turned and looked into his eyes, and he wanted to tell her that it was time she started to feel good—and that he was the man to help.

~ ~ ~

When the cab pulled up outside the lodge, Izzy jumped out, and Diego quickly followed her.

Audrey couldn't help but wonder if Izzy had been completely honest about her lack of interest in Diego. There seemed to be quite a spark between them, and although Izzy played it off that they were just doing whatever it took to give her and Ted a chance, she'd guess that there was more to it than that.

They all stood at the bottom of the steps that led up to the lobby.

"A drink in the bar, then?" asked Ted.

Audrey nodded and looked at the others.

Izzy slipped her arm through Diego's. "I'm afraid I'm absolutely pooped."

Diego faked a big yawn. "I also am too tired."

Audrey exchanged a glance with Ted, and he laughed. "Can you make it any more obvious, guys?"

Izzy laughed. "You're the one who isn't going along the with it. We tried. You two go ahead. Have a drink; we'll see you tomorrow."

Audrey's heart began to pound in her chest. She wasn't nervous; at least, she hadn't thought she was until now.

Diego took hold of her hand and kissed the back of it. "It was a pleasure to meet you, Audrey."

It was an over-the-top kind of gesture, one that Audrey would normally think of as comical, but when Diego did it, she could understand why Natalee had been so flustered.

"It was lovely to meet you, too."

Ted smiled at Izzy.

She waved a hand. "No need to say anything. I'll see you tomorrow."

Ted laughed and moved closer to Audrey as they watched the two of them walk inside.

Audrey's heart was still racing, and when he turned to look at her, she understood why; it wasn't nerves—she was excited!

"Are you okay with this?"

She nodded. "I am. I think they could have been a little more subtle about it, but ... I guess we're all grown-ups, and at least, we know that we have good friends who care about us."

"We do. I was thinking about that as we listened to them chatter on the ride back here. If nothing else, we have similar taste in friends."

Audrey laughed. "They're a pair together, aren't they?"

"Definitely." He offered her his hand. "But I have to say, I'm more interested in talking about you than talking about them. Do you want to go to the bar and get that drink?"

She sucked in a deep breath. Izzy's words earlier had stuck with her. She'd told her to go for a romantic walk on the beach, and that sounded so good. She hadn't done anything like that since before she met Richard—and that was more years ago than she cared to count.

Ted's smile faded. "Or would you rather call it a night?"

She caught his hand and shook her head rapidly. "No! I was wondering if you'd like to go for a walk on the beach? It's such a pretty night." There. She'd suggested it. Even if she never saw him again, at least he'd be that wonderful man she'd taken a romantic walk with.

He nodded happily. "I'd love to. I walk down there every morning when I'm here."

"Do you come here often?" She laughed as soon as the words came out of her mouth. "Sorry, that sounds like a cheesy pickup line."

"I was hoping it was one."

She looked up into his eyes, and he stopped walking. Her breath caught somewhere in her chest when he put his hands on her shoulders. He had such a kind smile, and his eyes ... she felt as though he really saw her—and that he liked what he saw.

She couldn't help it; she stepped closer to him.

He looked down at her lips and then back into her eyes. He didn't need to speak, the question hung in the air between them. She nodded and closed her eyes as his fingers slid over her cheek and into her hair.

His lips were warm and soft as they brushed over hers. It was the slightest touch, but it ignited something inside her, and she clung to him as the tentative kiss became something more. She'd never been kissed like that in her life. It started out slow and sweet and turned into something deep and passionate. Somehow, he made her feel sexy and safe all at the same time, like he would ravage her and defend her—and as she clung to him, she longed for him to do both.

~ ~ ~

When Ted finally lifted his head, he looked down into her eyes and tightened his arms around her.

"Damn," he breathed.

She shook her head in wonder. "Yeah, something like that, though, I think wow was the word I was going to go for."

He brushed her hair away from her face. "You're a beautiful woman, Audrey."

"Thank you." She looked away and then looked back at him. "You make me feel beautiful."

His heart clenched in his chest as he guessed that was a feeling she hadn't had in her marriage. "That's good to know, but you don't need anyone else to do it for you. You need to know—need to believe it. Beautiful is not a title someone else can bestow upon you, or ever take away from you. It's who you are."

A look of doubt crossed her face.

He dropped another kiss on her lips. "I'm not sweet-talking you, if that's what you're thinking. I'm simply telling you the truth."

"Thank you."

He could tell that she was struggling to believe him. Whether that was because she didn't see herself as beautiful or because she doubted his motives for saying it didn't really matter. He knew better than to push it. He took hold of her hand and continued on their walk, leading her down the path between the trees. A few minutes later they were out on the beach.

She was right when she'd said it was a pretty night. The sky was clear, and a million stars twinkled overhead. The moon was still low in the sky, and it illuminated a shining path across the lake. He turned to look at Audrey and smiled when he saw the expression on her face.

"It's so beautiful," she exclaimed. "I wanted to come out here the moment we arrived but hadn't had the chance yet."

"I'm glad I get to be the one who shows it to you for the first time. It's a beautiful place, and this evening is perfect."

She looked up into his eyes. "It is."

Part of him wanted to believe that she meant being here with him was perfect. But she was only talking about the moonlight, he was sure.

They walked hand in hand down to the water's edge. He felt so comfortable with her that they'd walked quite a way before Ted realized that maybe he should be making conversation.

"How do Ally and Brayden know Summer Lake, if you've never been before?"

"They came up here with a group of friends last summer and fell in love with the place. And," she smiled, "they ran into Eddie here. Apparently, they've known him for years."

"Do you know how?" Ted was curious about that.

Audrey shrugged. "I don't know. Perhaps because of the band? Ally sings sometimes. How long has Eddie been here?"

"A few years now."

"I bet you miss him, don't you? I'm lucky that Ally and Brayden both live in Ventura most of the time."

Ted nodded. It didn't seem right to explain his history with Eddie yet. He'd come to terms with the mistakes that he'd made, and he wasn't avoiding talking about it. But it was more important on this first date—at least, he hoped it was the first—to talk about her and get to know her better. "We've grown closer in the last few years than we've ever been. I try to get up here as often as I can. Eddie's fiancée, April, is a wonderful young woman, and her son Marcus …" He smiled. "He may not be blood, but he's my grandson."

"Aww. That's wonderful. I'm looking forward to the day I get to have grandbabies. I'm not holding my breath though. Neither of my two are in a hurry."

"They have time."

She laughed. "They do. I'm the impatient one."

He slid his arm around her shoulders as they walked. "What do you do for fun?"

"I work a lot. Izzy and I go out to dinner. I meet up the with kids when they have time." She shrugged. "I suppose I'm a boring old fart really, oh, but I do love to walk on the beach."

He hugged her into his side. "How dare you call my new girlfriend a boring old fart?"

He meant it as a joke, and almost wished he could take it back when her eyes widened in surprise. He didn't want her to think he was coming on too strong.

To his relief, she laughed. "It's sweet of you to stand up for her, but you don't know her very well."

He raised an eyebrow. "I'll bet that if she gives me the chance to get to know her, I'll be able to prove that she's not boring at all."

"Oh, yeah?" She raised her chin.

"Yeah." He held her gaze, hoping that she would give him the chance.

"Well, if you're still interested in seeing each other again after this evening ..."

"I am. Are you?"

"Yes." There was no hesitation when she answered. He got the impression that she was as attracted to him as he was to her. And it was something more than just physical.

"Good. What are you doing tomorrow?"

She sighed. "I'm sorry. I'm having lunch with the kids before they leave, and I'll no doubt spend the morning with Izzy."

"That's okay. I'm spending time with Eddie and the family, too. But not in the evening. Do you want to have dinner with me?"

Her smile was back. "I'd love to."

"Great."

She shivered, and for the first time, he realized that she must be cold. He took his jacket off and wrapped it around her shoulders. "I'm sorry. I should have thought."

She dropped her gaze and then looked up at him through long lashes. "Don't apologize, please. I ... I hadn't noticed the cold until just now. I'm feeling all warm and fuzzy."

He chuckled. "The champagne must be wearing off."

"It wasn't the champagne."

He closed his arms around her. "No?"

"No. It's you."

He couldn't help but pull her in for another kiss. She was so open and honest. He got the feeling that she was way out of her comfort zone, that she wasn't used to being with a man, but she wasn't hiding anything or being shy. Her lips were full and soft, and they opened up to him willingly. He shifted his hips away from her at the thought of her opening up for him and letting him in. He wanted to hold her closer, press himself into her softness, but he knew that might be too much. They were going to see each other again; there was no hurry. He knew it would be better to take his time—even if the ache in his pants begged to differ.

When they finally came up for air, he'd swear he saw desire in her eyes, but he forced himself to ignore it. Instead, he took hold of her hand and started leading her back toward the path that would take them back to the lodge.

"We should get back. It's late, and you're cold."

She looked as though she was about to protest, but instead, she nodded. "You're right."

He saw her back to her room, promising himself the whole way that he would see her safely inside and leave her there.

"Goodnight, Audrey."

She searched his face and he could tell she was wondering what he was thinking.

He cupped her face between his hands. "Just so we're clear; I'm forcing myself to be a gentleman. I'm not saying goodnight because I want to, but because it's the right thing to do."

"What if I don't want to say goodnight yet?"

His heart leaped into his throat, and the ache in his pants intensified. He closed his eyes and dropped a kiss on her lips. "You'll make it even harder for me to walk away, but it's still the right thing to do."

She smiled and nodded. "You're a good man, Ted."

He had to laugh, and then he had to explain. "Sorry. It's just that's one of Diego's little sayings. A good man is hard to find—and a hard man is good to find."

She laughed with him. "I'll have to take your word for that."

"You've found one."

"Will I find him again tomorrow?"

He nodded.

"Okay. In that case. I'll say goodnight."

He backed her against the door and kissed her deeply. He didn't want to leave her with any doubt about the fact that he wanted her.

She certainly left him with no doubt that it was mutual. Eventually, she pulled away and gave him what he could only describe as a wicked smile. "I'll see you tomorrow, then."

"Tomorrow." He stood staring at her door for a few moments after she'd gone in. It'd be so easy to knock and go in with her. He adjusted his pants and turned away with a sigh. Easy wasn't always best, though—in any sense.

Chapter Seven

Audrey woke early on Sunday morning as she usually did. She rolled over and looked out of the window at the lake and the mountains, still gray in the early morning light. It was so beautiful here.

She sat up and piled the pillows behind her then hugged her knees to her chest with a smile. She felt beautiful here. Though, that had a lot to do with Ted. She reached up and touched her lips, remembering the way he'd kissed her. To use his own word—damn! He was a good kisser.

She felt as though she was still a little worse off for the champagne. She felt a little light-headed and tingly. Perhaps it was the champagne, or perhaps, as she'd told him last night, it was Ted. She closed her eyes and could see his face. He was gorgeous! He had such kind eyes and his smile ... She sighed. What was happening to her? She was like a young girl, sitting in here in bed swooning over the guy she'd met last night.

At least, she hadn't been like a young irresponsible girl. She hadn't brought him home with her. Well, to be fair, that was down to him, not her. If he'd made any attempt to come in with her, she would have willingly brought him to her bed. A rush of heat coursed through her at the thought. Part of her wished that she'd taken his hand and brought him in. If she had, he'd be here now, lying beside her.

That thought gave her pause. She hadn't woken up next to a man in four years. She hadn't woken up next to anyone other than Richard in more than thirty years. Wow. That was a long time. Was she ready to change it? She bit down on her bottom lip but couldn't help smiling. Yes. She was.

She rolled out of bed and popped a pod in the coffee maker. It was hard to believe that this time yesterday she hadn't even known he existed. Now, she was wondering if he was in the gym again. She'd love to go and see but wouldn't allow herself to. They'd arranged to have dinner this evening. She could wait until then.

She wrapped up in her robe and took her coffee out onto the balcony. It was too cold to stay out for long, but she wanted to enjoy the fresh air and the view. As she snuggled deeper into her robe, she smiled at the memory of him taking off his jacket and wrapping it around her. He was a true gentleman. She couldn't help but compare him with Richard; he'd always refused to give her his coat when she was cold, telling her that she should have prepared better and brought her own.

She went back inside with a smile. Richard was the past, and she wasn't so naïve as to think that Ted was the future, but he was at least a sign that the future could be so much brighter.

She jumped when the phone on the bedside table rang and rushed toward it, filled with hope that it might be Ted.

"Hello?"

"Hey, are you alone?" It was Izzy.

"Yes. What are you doing up?"

"I've been asking myself that for the last half hour. I think I'm just too excited to hear what happened with you last night. So…?"

Audrey chuckled. "So, what?"

"So, did you?"

"We walked on the beach, yes."

"Ugh! That's not what I mean, and you know it. Are you decent? I'll be there in a minute."

Audrey hung up and went to the door. Izzy was only down the hall, and it was only a few moments before she knocked.

"So, tell me all about it," she demanded before Audrey had even closed the door behind her.

"He's wonderful."

Izzy waggled her eyebrows. "In bed?"

"No!"

"Aww. I was hoping that you two got it on."

Audrey laughed. "Got it on? That sounds awful."

"You know what I mean." Izzy rolled her eyes. "What do you want me to say? That he made mad passionate love to you?"

"Hmm, that sounds good."

"It does? Awesome? So, even though you didn't, you would?"

"You're terrible, do you know this?"

Izzy nodded happily. "I should. You tell me often enough. But that's beside the point. Answer the question."

Audrey took a sip of her coffee and smiled at her friend over the rim of her mug. "Okay. Honestly? I would … I wanted to … and I'm hoping we will."

"Damn, girlfriend! Yay! There's hope for you yet!"

"Thanks. I think. Had you given up hope?"

"Not quite but I was starting to think that you might die an old maid."

"So was I, but …"

"But Ted has reminded you what it feels like to be a woman?"

She nodded slowly. "Yes, I guess that's about it. More than that though. He didn't just make me feel like a woman, he made me feel beautiful ... sexy."

"Oh, Audrey!" Izzy came and hugged her. "That's wonderful. This couldn't be more perfect, could it? You're here for the week with nothing but time on your hands. He's here for the week, too. It's a beautiful place, you're both away from home and ..." She sat down on the bed. "You have two super-king-sized beds to choose from every night. I hope you're going to make the most of it."

Audrey tried to hide her smile but couldn't. "I hope so, too."

"You have to keep me posted all week. I want to know what's going on the whole time, you hear me?"

"I'll check in, but I might not share all the details."

She expected Izzy to protest, but instead she smiled.

"What, you're not going to demand more?"

"Nope. The very fact that you said that tells me that you're expecting things to happen and you don't want to bonk and tell."

Audrey laughed. "Isn't it supposed to be kiss and tell?"

"Not in this case, no. Come on though I want to hear about last night. What did you do after we left you? You can tell me all about it, and then we can go and get some breakfast. I'm starving."

~ ~ ~

Ted looked around as he took his seat next to Marcus. They usually came to the Boathouse for breakfast on the weekends, but Eddie had suggested they should do lunch today instead.

"Looking for someone?" asked Eddie. The gleam in his eye made Ted suspect that he knew exactly who he was looking for—and why they were here now instead of earlier. He tried to hide a guilty smile.

"You tell me."

Eddie grasped his shoulder. "Honestly. I don't know, but I'm hoping that you might be looking for Ally's mom."

He nodded, not sure what he should say.

April smiled at him. She looked pleased.

"Who's Ally?" asked Marcus.

"An old friend of mine," said Eddie. "And Grandad is friends with her mom."

Marcus looked up at Ted. "I didn't know you had friends here."

"I don't. She doesn't live here; she's just visiting for the week."

"The week?" Eddie raised an eyebrow. "I didn't know that. I thought they were leaving today."

Ted's heart sank. He didn't want his son thinking that he was staying here because of Audrey. "Ally and Brayden are leaving today. But Audrey's taking some time off. I didn't know that until last night."

Eddie smiled. "It's okay. I was worried about you staying the whole week, thinking you'd be at a loose end most of the time. I'm glad you'll have someone to hang out with."

Ted smiled back. Most of the time he felt like he didn't deserve Eddie.

"Can we invite her over for dinner one night?" asked April.

"I don't know." Ted looked at her and then at Eddie and Marcus. He'd missed out on too many years of his son's life. He knew how lucky he was to be included in it now and he didn't want to mess anything up by not being completely honest with all of them. He winked at Marcus. "Don't laugh at me. I know I'm a bit old for this, but I'm kind of hoping that she's going to be …" He hesitated to say it.

"Your girlfriend?" Marcus asked.

He nodded and they all smiled at him.

"That's awesome, Grandad. You should bring her over for dinner. Are you going to marry her?"

He had to laugh. "Slow down at bit. I'm getting ahead of myself thinking of her as my girlfriend. We don't really know each other yet. I'm going to have dinner with her tonight, since I know you guys are busy, but from there ... I don't know what will happen." He turned to April. "I'd love to bring her for dinner if she wants to come, but ..."

"I totally understand. I'll keep my fingers crossed for you. Just know that you're welcome if you want to bring her. And we understand if you don't—and if you get the chance to spend time with her, know that we understand that, too."

"No. I'm here this week to spend time with you guys. You come first."

Eddie nodded. He understood. "Whatever works best for you, Dad ... there she is."

Ted turned and saw her walking out onto the deck with Izzy and her children. His smile faded when he saw Richard following not far behind.

Eddie caught his gaze. "Don't tell me you're jealous?"

"No! I just don't like the man. It sounded as though she didn't have the best life with him."

April looked over and nodded. "I don't like the look of him. He's mean. You can tell just from his mouth and his eyes."

Ted felt the same way, and he was glad of their support, but he was here to have lunch with them, not to sit here watching Audrey. She glanced over and caught his gaze. He lifted his hand and smiled. The way she smiled back at him made his heart race.

April nudged him with her elbow. "I don't think you need to doubt whether she's interested in you."

He shook his head happily. She was obviously as pleased to see him as he was her. He was looking forward to this evening, but that didn't mean he wasn't going to enjoy the afternoon with his family.

When they'd finished eating, Eddie nodded to where Audrey was sitting. "I'd like to say goodbye to Ally and Brayden on the way out. April didn't get to see them last night."

Ted nodded. He was more than happy to stop by their table.

"Can I wait for you at the truck?" asked Marcus.

April nodded. "You can, but don't go off, okay?"

"Sure."

Ted watched him saunter away and smiled. "He's come a long way in the few years I've known him," he told April.

"He's grown up so much." To his surprise, she gave him a hug. "I hope you know how grateful I am."

"Eddie's the one who's made the difference in his life."

"He is, and Marcus loves him so much. But you helped us all. And you've made us a family. He loves you, too, you know. And so do I."

Ted hugged her into his side. He was moved. He had helped them out when they first got together, and April's ex-husband had been threatening them. He knew April appreciated what he'd done, but this was the first time she'd ever said she loved him.

He had to clear his throat before he spoke. "I love you, too, April."

Eddie caught his eye and nodded, and Ted felt as though his heart might overflow.

He jumped when a hand came down on his shoulder. "I thought I'd find you here. I'm almost ready to leave," said Diego.

"Do you want to come and say goodbye to Audrey before you go—and Izzy?"

Diego chuckled. "I'm on my way to bid the lovely Audrey farewell."

Ted raised an eyebrow. "Not Izzy?" He couldn't help but wonder what might have happened last night.

"Not yet. I'm giving her a ride home."

"I see."

"No. You don't. It's just a ride."

"Which you offered out of the goodness of your heart and not in the hope of impressing her by taking her in your private jet?"

"Ted, Ted. When will you understand that when I wish to impress a woman, I don't use the jet?"

His son, Zack, appeared by his side and laughed. "It's true. You know it's true."

Ted had to laugh. "Okay. But I don't think we need to discuss what you do use—not in front of a lady." He gave April an apologetic smile, but she just laughed. "I'm going to talk to Ally. I'm staying out of this."

They all followed her across the deck of the restaurant to where Audrey's family were sitting. Audrey got to her feet and came to Ted.

He couldn't help it; he smiled at Richard as he pecked her cheek. "We're leaving, and I wanted to say goodbye to Ally and Brayden." He felt as though he needed to explain why he'd come over.

"And I have come to tell Miss Isobel that her chariot awaits whenever she is ready," Diego announced.

Ted and Audrey both turned to see what Izzy's reaction would be.

"Can you call it a chariot when it has wings?" she asked.

Ally grinned at Diego. "You're flying her home?"

"I could hardly leave her behind."

Audrey chuckled beside Ted and he raised an eyebrow at her. "Tell me you see what's going on here? It's not just me, is it?" she asked in a low voice.

"I thought it was just me. Diego insists she's not interested."

"So, does she. But I'm not buying it. Are you?"

He shook his head. "Not for a minute." He spotted April watching them and smiled at her. "Audrey this is my daughter-in-law, April."

April stepped forward with a smile. "It's lovely to meet you."

"You, too," said Audrey.

"I told Ted already, but I'll tell you as well. You have an open invite to come over for dinner any time you like this week—but no pressure to come if you're both too busy."

Ted glanced sideways at Audrey, wondering how she'd feel to know that he'd already told April and Eddie that they planned to see each other this week. To his relief, she looked happy about it.

"That's so sweet of you. Thank you. I don't know what we're planning yet—"

"You're here for the week?"

They all turned to see Richard standing there. Ted was tempted to say yes, *we* are. But it wasn't his place to say it. He was happy when Audrey did.

"We are. Are you leaving today?"

Richard nodded. "I have client meetings tomorrow." He smiled at Ted and offered him his card. "Feel free to give me a call whenever you're looking for any ad help."

Ted took the card and looked at it. "Thanks, but Audrey has me covered."

Richard's smile faded. "I see."

Ally came and wrapped her arms around Audrey. "You guys have a great time this week. Call me when you get home, won't you?" She smiled at Ted. "It's my turn to have you both over for dinner."

Ted recovered quickly. He knew she was making a point to her father. He didn't know why she felt the need to do that, but he was happy to play along. He gave her a hug. "Thanks, Ally. We'll call you when we land."

Richard scowled at Audrey. "You're flying home, too?"

She looked at Ted. "Are we?"

He nodded. He didn't see any reason why not. "We are." He smiled pleasantly at Richard. "It makes life that much easier, don't you think?"

Richard nodded.

Ted wasn't normally one to play one-upmanship like that, and he didn't feel great about it, but the way Ally smiled at him made it worth it.

He turned and kissed Audrey's cheek one more time—for no-one's benefit but his own. "I'll see you later."

She nodded and held his gaze for a moment. She was silently thanking him, and any guilty feelings he'd had about Richard melted away. He'd do anything to see her smile at him like that.

Chapter Eight

Audrey set her book down on the table and stared out at the lake. It had been a beautiful afternoon and, after she'd said goodbye to the kids and Izzy, she'd come back over here to the lodge to make the most of it. She had plans to hike and drive around the area and even do some shopping at the plaza while she was here, but this afternoon was the first time she'd had to herself in weeks. She'd changed into her shorts and brought her book out onto the balcony. Sitting in the sun and reading was one of her favorite things to do.

It was getting a little chillier now, and she went inside to get her sweatshirt and poured herself a glass of pineapple juice to take back outside. She noticed that her phone was flashing; she'd plugged it in to charge and forgotten about it. That wasn't like her. She picked it up, feeling a momentary dread that something might have happened—that someone needed her and hadn't been able to get hold of her.

There were two voicemails—one from Izzy and one from Ally—and a text from Ted. She checked on her daughter first.

"Hey, Mom. I just wanted to say thanks again for coming this weekend." Ally laughed. "And also, you're welcome! Ted's awesome! I want to hear all about it. And tell him from me that he's a star for going along with me in front of Dad. I know you'll say you don't want to hear it, but Dad's pissed! He is sooo freaking jealous. He's jealous that you found someone so much better than him. But he's jealous that someone else gets to be with you, too. He's an idiot, and I think he's just starting to figure that out. Anyway. Call me when you get a chance. If you don't, then have lots of fun and call me when you get back. Oh, and sorry if I put you on the spot by saying I expect to see you both when you get back. Sorry, but also not sorry. I'd say Ted was pretty happy about it. Okay. Gotta run. Love you. Call me."

Audrey smiled to herself. That was typical Ally. All over the place and full of love. She'd call her later to make sure that she'd gotten home okay.

She checked Izzy's message next.

"Hey, you! Just letting you know that I'm home. Don't worry about work this week. I have it covered. I promise you. You enjoy yourself. Have fun with Ted—and keep me posted. If you don't call me, I'll only call you, and you know what a wonderful sense of timing I have. Seriously, Audrey. I hope you have a blast this week. Love you, girlfriend. Talk soon."

"Oh, I'll be calling you, *Miss Isobel.*" Audrey told her phone. "You just flew home in a private jet with a very handsome man, and you didn't even mention anything about it in your voicemail? Ha!"

She sucked in a deep breath and clicked on the text message from Ted.

I hope you enjoyed your day. The highlight of mine was seeing you at lunch time. Meet me in the lobby at seven?

She pressed her lips together but couldn't hold in her smile. To her amazement, butterflies were swirling in her tummy. She hugged her phone to her chest, then set it down hurriedly,

feeling stupid. She wasn't a girl! She was a grown woman—
with a daughter who was too old to behave like that. Still, it
was a nice feeling. Butterflies and excitement at the thought of
going on a date—that was something she hadn't thought she'd
experience again in her life.

She picked the phone back up and tapped out a reply.

I can't wait.

She looked at it for a few moments and then deleted it.

I'm looking forward to it.

She frowned. That didn't seem enthusiastic enough. She
deleted that, too, and stared at the screen. Then she let out a
little laugh. This was ridiculous!

I can't wait.

That was the truth, and she wasn't one for playing games. If
it was too much, it was too much, but it was her truth, and that
was all she could go with.

~ ~ ~

Ted checked himself over in the mirror and nodded. He'd
do. He wore a black shirt and black jeans. This place was
casual. He hoped that Audrey hadn't gone to any great effort.
He rubbed his cheek. Perhaps he should shave? He didn't want
to. The guy in the mirror gave him a rueful smile. He'd heard
April telling Eddie that he didn't need to shave, because he
looked sexier with a bit of *scruff.* If he was honest, Ted was
hoping that he could maybe work the same angle on Audrey.

He'd been a clean-shaven kind of guy ever since … he
stopped and thought about it and his smile disappeared. Since
he went to work in the city after he and Irene had separated.
He blew out a sigh. He didn't need to be thinking about that.

In one respect, Irene cheating on him and telling him that she wanted a divorce had been the best thing that had ever happened to him. It had changed him and changed his life. He'd gone into business for himself, met Diego and gone into partnership with him and career and money-wise had never looked back. But he had one big regret. He'd never looked back at Eddie either. He'd left his son behind.

He went back out into the bedroom and stood before the windows looking out at the lake. That had been the hardest thing he'd ever done. He'd believed he was doing it for the right reasons, but ... He shook his head. You can't change the past. He knew that. He pulled himself together. The only place you ever get to live is in the present. And he knew he was doing a good job of making up for his mistakes.

He checked his watch. He had a good feeling about tonight ... a good feeling about Audrey. He liked the idea of making the most of the present with her. He didn't need to look back at the past; he just needed to enjoy tonight, enjoy this week— and try to hold himself back from wondering whether this was something that might have a future.

He'd said that he'd meet her in the lobby at seven. It was only six-thirty. He picked up his phone with a smile and tapped out a text.

Did you mean it when you said you couldn't wait?

He waited for a reply, wondering if she was perhaps getting ready and wouldn't even see his message.

Of course. I don't say things I don't mean. Why?

He wasn't one to insert emojis in his texts, but he found one that was winking and sent that first, then hurried to tap out.

Because I can't either. I'm ready whenever you are.

His phone rang and he hit answer with a smile.

She laughed. "Are you serious? You're ready now?"

"Yes, ma'am. But I can wait. I'm not trying to hurry you."

She laughed again. "You're not. I've been sitting here for ten minutes wondering if I should go for a walk while I wait."

He laughed with her. "Maybe we should … go take a walk around the plaza"

"I'd love to. See you in the lobby?"

"I'll be right there."

He grabbed his room key and wallet from the counter and hurried to the door. He wanted to get there first, not leave her standing around waiting for him.

He was glad the elevator arrived almost as soon as he pressed the button. He hurried across the lobby and stood near the reception desk where he had a full view of both elevators and would see her the minute she arrived.

"Evening, Mr. Rawlins."

"Oh, hi Roxy. How are you?"

"Great thanks. Almost ready to go home. Are you off out for the evening?"

He nodded, keeping one eye on the elevators.

Roxy gave him a knowing smile. "You have a date … don't you?"

He nodded, not sure that this was a conversation he wanted to have. He liked Roxy. She was friends with Eddie and April, but he wasn't one to discuss his personal life.

She covered her mouth with her hand and looked at him with wide eyes. "I am so sorry! It's none of my business. I'll shut up." She smiled. "It's only because I'm so surprised … and so happy for you! Who … oh, shoot. Ignore me. I'm sorry."

He had to laugh. It wasn't like her to be so unprofessional, and he could see that she was genuinely pleased for him. He waved a hand at her. "Don't worry about it. I'm not annoyed with you." He winked at her. "I'm nervous!"

She grinned. "You have no reason on earth to be nervous. Whoever she is, she's a lucky lady."

Ted drew in a deep breath when Audrey emerged from the elevator. She'd looked amazing in the dress she'd worn last night—classy, elegant and sexy all rolled into one. Tonight, she looked like a breath of fresh air. She wore jeans and a white top with long sleeves and lacy edges. It was a simple outfit, but finished with red heels and gold jewelry. She was breath-taking.

"Oh, she's lovely!" He heard Roxy speak beside him but didn't take his eyes off Audrey—he couldn't.

She smiled when she spotted him, and when she reached him, he greeted her with a hug. She even smelled wonderful. He didn't know what it was, but he breathed her in as he pecked her cheek.

"You look wonderful."

"Thank you, so do you." He loved the way she let her gaze rove over him, and got the impression that his choice of outfit met with her approval, too.

"Shall we?" He offered her his arm, and she took it with a smile.

"Aww!"

Ted shot a quick glance at Roxy who was watching them with a big silly smile on her face. He winked at her, and she grinned back at him and held up her thumbs.

Audrey turned, too, and Roxy made a big show of lifting her thumbs up toward her hair as she pushed it back behind her shoulders.

"Oh, hi, Roxy. I thought you were off until tomorrow."

"I was supposed to be, but I had to cover for a little while." She smiled. "I don't mind. In fact, I'm glad I was here for this."

"For what?" Audrey gave her a puzzled look, and Ted had to laugh.

"To see us go out on a date," he explained. "I was just telling Roxy how nervous and excited I am. I didn't know she knows you, too."

"Aww." Ted wasn't sure if it was Audrey or Roxy who made the sound this time, but judging by the look on Audrey's face it didn't matter—it was a good thing.

~ ~ ~

The butterflies swirled in Audrey's tummy as they walked down the steps in front of the lodge. If someone had told her even this time yesterday, that she'd be out on a date this evening she would have laughed at them. She would have laughed even harder if they'd said that she'd be out with a very good-looking man whom she felt completely at ease with.

He turned to look at her as they reached the bottom of the steps. "How was your day?"

"It was good thanks. After we saw you at the Boathouse, I saw the kids off … and Izzy." She smiled. "Have you heard from Diego?"

"No." Ted smirked. He knew what she was getting at. "Have you heard from Izzy?"

"She called to let me know that she was home and reminded me that I'm supposed to be taking a break from work this week and that she has everything covered."

"No mention of her trip home, or Diego?"

"Not a word—which in itself, speaks volumes. I'm just not sure what it says."

"I think they'd make a great match," said Ted.

"They do seem well suited, but perhaps what we're seeing is just that they're similar?"

"Perhaps." Ted smiled. "Only time will tell. Do you think that being similar means they're not well-suited?"

Audrey thought about that. "Not necessarily."

"Good."

She looked up at him as they reached the main square in the plaza. "Why's that?"

"Because, from the little I know so far, I'd say that we're similar."

"You would?"

"Yes. Diego and Izzy are outgoing, whereas you and I ... we're much less so."

"True. I don't see you as being reserved though."

"I'm not. I just prefer to observe. I see more than I say."

She smiled. "Then we are similar. I tend to live inside my own head. I don't need to be the center of attention; I'm happier being the glue that holds things together."

He squeezed her hand. "Are you truly happier in that role, or is it just what you've gotten used to?"

She thought about that. "Honestly? I don't know. I am used to it. It's part of being a working mom. You take care of everything, of everyone. You make sure that the kids have what they need and the office is running as it should ..." She shrugged. "I've never really questioned it before."

"And who takes care of you?"

"I do."

He raised an eyebrow. "And how much time and energy do you put into that?"

She laughed. "Whatever's left over. And besides, it's not like the kids are at home anymore. They've been out on their own for years now. And for the last few years, I've been on my own." She gave him a puzzled look. "What are you getting at?"

"I'm not getting at anything, just trying to get to know you." He smiled.

"Well, going back to the question of if we're similar, I'd say that we probably are. I might be less outgoing than Izzy—but to be fair, that's not hard—but I'm not some poor little wallflower. I'm driven, in business, and in most things. I'd guess that you are, too."

"Absolutely. I don't see you as a wallflower. You couldn't be one if you tried; you're too beautiful for that. I just wondered if you've gotten used to putting yourself last. And only because I'd hate for that to be the case."

"No. Well, maybe. To be honest, I've been lost for a while. But remember last night? Izzy told you we were celebrating my new beginning? That was because ... because it's finally dawned on me that I'm not who I used to be. I suppose that's what you're talking about. I don't have any of the roles I used to have. I get to do and be whatever I want now."

He held her gaze for a moment. "It took you a long time to get over your divorce?"

The question surprised her, but she didn't mind him asking. "It's not that so much as it took me a long time to get over losing who I was. I struggled a bit when the twins went to college, but I'd had time to get used to that. And then ... Richard ... we hadn't been close for a long time, but I was used to being his wife, you know?"

He nodded, but she wasn't sure that he could understand.

She let out a nervous laugh. "I thought first dates were supposed to be light and fun. Why on earth am I rambling on about my life?"

"Because I asked you. I'm sorry. I didn't mean to ..." He frowned. "I'm sorry. It's just that ..." He met her gaze and smiled. "Apparently, I'm not very good at this dating thing."

She raised an eyebrow. "Don't tell me you don't date. I won't believe you."

He dropped his gaze and smiled. "I do date, but not ... I date because Diego drags me along mostly. It's easier to go out and have a few drinks or dinner than it is to have him nag me about it."

She had to laugh. "Well, there's a difference between us. Izzy tries to do the same with me, but I don't let her."

He looked serious now. "When was the last time you went on a date?"

Her heart hammered in her chest. Did she really want to admit the truth to him? She looked into his eyes. She couldn't find the right word to describe what she saw in them, but it was something that she trusted. She blew out a sigh. "If you really want to know, it's been ..." She did the math in her head; it wasn't something she'd ever wanted to put a number to before. She made a face when she figured it out. "Thirty-three years."

A look of surprised crossed his face, but he recovered quickly.

"Does that make things awkward?" she asked. "I feel kind of embarrassed."

He stopped walking and slid his arms around her waist, pulling her to him and looking down into her eyes.

She smiled nervously, wondering what he was going to say.

"It doesn't make things awkward; it just makes this even more important."

"This? Tonight?"

He nodded and dropped a kiss on her lips. "Tonight, tomorrow, this week, and after we leave." He dropped another kiss on her lips. "You and me."

She let herself sag against him. All she was letting herself think about was tonight. She was trying not to think about the rest of the week—she didn't want to get too carried away. She wanted to protest that he didn't even know her, but she couldn't help feeling that somehow, he did, just as she felt as though she knew him.

He held her gaze. "Too much?"

She shook her head slowly. She knew she should tell him that it was, but she didn't want to.

Chapter Nine

Ted looked around the terrace. He enjoyed eating out here when the weather was nice enough. There were a dozen tables and a stone balustrade with a beautiful view of the lake and the mountains beyond.

He'd thought it would be quiet this evening. Being a Sunday night and still early in the season, he'd assumed that they might have the terrace to themselves. He'd been wrong. When the waiter had led them out here, almost all the tables were occupied. Ted was glad that he'd requested this table specifically. It had the best view.

He got to his feet when Audrey came back from the ladies' room. She took his breath away every time he laid eyes on her. He knew he'd probably scared her off a little earlier, talking the way he had as they walked over at the plaza, but he just couldn't help himself. She had his head turned right around, and he was thinking all kinds of things, he shouldn't be. He'd promised himself that he'd keep it lighter over dinner, and he'd managed to, but now the end of the evening was looming, and he got the impression that she was nervous about what might come next.

Once she was seated, she looked around. "This place is quite something, isn't it?"

"It is. They've done a great job with the lodge and the restaurant. It's hard to believe that it's only been here a couple of years."

"It has? I didn't know that."

"Yes. It hadn't opened the first time I came to visit Eddie and April. I stayed at the resort in town. It's a great place—for what it is, but I'm more comfortable here."

"I'm the same. I looked at the resort and might have stayed there if it was just for the weekend, but since Izzy insisted that I take the week off, I thought I'd feel more at home here."

He reached across the table and took hold of her hand. "I'll have to thank Izzy." He wondered if he was saying too much too soon again, but she smiled.

"Me too. Just think, we probably wouldn't have met."

He smiled. "We would. I would have seen you in the Boathouse last night and introduced myself."

She laughed. "Then maybe I shouldn't thank Izzy. That would have been preferable to you catching me gawking at you through the window in the gym."

He laughed. "I'll never forget that. That was the first time I ever saw you."

She made a face. "Yes. And I was still a bleary-eyed mess, and I didn't even notice you at first."

He gave her a sad look. "You didn't?"

She laughed. "You know I didn't. I didn't expect anyone to be there, so I didn't notice that there was. But when I did see you ..." She waggled her eyebrows.

"What?" he asked, liking this new playful side to her.

She pressed her lips together and shrugged.

"What? You can't say that and then leave me hanging. When you did see me ... what?"

Her cheeks flushed, but she met his gaze. "Let's just say I liked what I saw."

"Good to know. I liked what I saw, too."

She laughed. "Now you're just being kind. I was a mess! I hadn't even had coffee yet."

"It's the truth. I thought you were beautiful."

"Then you must need your eyes tested. My hair was all over the place, I had no makeup on. I was wearing sweats ..."

He had to laugh. "I know. I saw you. And I promise you, I'm not blowing smoke up your skirt."

"Seriously?"

"If you don't believe me, you can ask Diego what I said."

"I'd rather you tell me yourself."

He could hardly get out of it now. He hoped that it would come across the way he meant it. "I told him that I'd seen a woman when I was in the gym, and that ..."

She watched him expectantly. There was laughter in her eyes.

"That we'd had a moment."

She nodded. "I thought that, too. But it does nothing to dispute the fact that I looked terrible."

There was nothing for it. "Okay. Don't take this the wrong way."

"I won't. I promise."

"I told him that you were a beautiful mess."

To his relief, she laughed. "Wow! I think that might be the best compliment I've ever had. It's certainly the most real."

He squeezed her hand. "I'm nothing, if not real."

"I can tell. I like that about you. What I don't understand is why someone like you isn't married or at least, taken. You're a good-looking guy, you're kind and ..." She shrugged, "successful. Did you never remarry after Eddie's mom?"

Ted's smile faded, and he shook his head. "I never wanted to. The only good thing that came out of my marriage was

Eddie and …" Damn. Was he really going to tell her what he'd done? It wasn't something he liked to think about, let alone explain to people he barely knew. But he felt as though he already knew her. And if he wanted to spend more time with her, if they wanted to explore what could happen between them, then he owed her this. She needed to know what kind of man he'd been.

Her smile had faded, too. "I'm sorry. I didn't mean to pry. Forget I asked. Do you want dessert?"

"Do you?"

She gave him a guilty smile. "I was hoping to get the cheesecake. We had some yesterday afternoon, and it's wonderful."

He smiled and caught the waiter's eye. He wasn't going to let himself off the hook; he was just using this diversion to gather his thoughts.

Once she had her cheesecake, he took a deep breath and nodded.

"You don't have to tell me anything you don't want to." She held her fork up to him and slid a bite of cheesecake into his mouth.

She was making it too easy to let the matter go, but he knew that if he let it slide, it'd only be harder to tell her about it in the future.

"You're right, that is good," he said. "But I do need to tell you about why I never remarried."

She shook her head.

"I want to," he insisted. "I want you to understand."

She set her fork down. "That sounds scary."

"I'm not proud of who I was."

"Tell me."

"Irene and I weren't well suited, but we had Eddie and so we tried to make it work. Irene liked to play us off against each other. She used to tell Eddie that I didn't have time for him—when all I was doing was working hard to support us. And then she met someone else. She saw him for almost a year before I found out." Ted closed his eyes and drew in a deep breath. It was still painful, even after all these years. "She managed to keep me in the dark, but Eddie knew the guy. And when she told me she wanted a divorce, she also told me that it was what Eddie wanted too—that he loved her new boyfriend and that the three of them were happy together."

Audrey shook her head sadly but didn't interrupt him.

"She also told Eddie that I didn't want him. She made us both believe that it was for the best if I just left the picture. The only thing she wanted from me was money—and I paid it willingly. Because, you see …" He turned and stared out at the lake before looking back at her. "The stupidest thing I ever did was to believe her. I believed that Eddie didn't want me in his life and that he was better off with his new stepdad. I want to tell you that I walked away purely for Eddie's benefit, but I can't. Part of it was because of my own hurt pride. My wife was rejecting me—that hurt but I could handle it. But my son as well?" He shook his head. "That hurt too much, and I walked away and never looked back."

Audrey squeezed his hand. "You must have looked back at some point. You and Eddie seem close now."

"Eddie looked me up after he turned thirty. For the first couple of years we had an uneasy truce. It wasn't until he and April got together, and I was able to help them through some trouble that we got close."

"Wow. I'm sorry you lost all that time in each other's lives."

"So am I. It's my own fault, though. I believed her lies, and I put my son through hell because of my own pride."

She gave him a puzzled look.

"She told me that Eddie loved the man she left me for. She told Eddie that I didn't want him, that I'd just walked out on them. And that man made Eddie's childhood a living hell."

"Oh. I'm so sorry."

"Thanks. I know it's not something to talk about on a first date, but I still hate what I did. I'm ashamed of myself, and I'd rather you know that about me before ..." He was doing it again, talking about a possible future already.

She squeezed his hand. "Thank you. I'm glad I know. But I don't think it's some dark secret about you. It's just a tough part of life that you went through. We all have those. Nobody's life is all sunshine and roses. We all have to weather some storms."

He had to smile. She made it sound like he wasn't quite the monster he still saw himself to be. "Thanks. What's that line? Into every life a little rain must fall?"

She smiled. "Longfellow; isn't it?"

"I think so."

"And there's a line in there about not clinging to the mouldering past. You might want to remember that part."

Ted had to smile. He was trying to recall the whole poem. "It sounds like good advice to me."

"It is. The whole thing is about how life isn't always great, but we can't get stuck in the dark parts."

"That's right." He remembered now. "Behind the clouds the sun is still shining."

"Exactly."

"Thanks, Audrey."

"I didn't do anything. Other than listen."

"That means more than you know."

Ted took hold of her hand as they were leaving. It made her smile. She might not have been on a first date in more than three decades, but she knew that this was how it was supposed to feel. The butterflies in her stomach still hadn't settled. They took to flight again every time he looked at her.

"Ted!"

They both turned at the sound of his name being called. Two couples sat together at the far end of the terrace, and one of the men raised his hand in greeting.

"Do you mind?" he asked.

"Of course not." If he didn't mind introducing her to his friends, it was fine by her.

The women smiled warmly at her when they reached the table. Audrey guessed that they were around her age—in their mid-fifties. One of the men looked very familiar, but she couldn't place him.

The other man spoke to Ted. "I didn't know you were here this weekend. It's good to see you."

"You, too." Ted smiled around at them. "All of you." He put his arm around Audrey and drew her forward. She hadn't done it intentionally, but she'd been lingering a little behind him.

"Audrey, I'd like you to meet some friends of mine. This is Seymour and Chris, and Clay and Marianne."

She smiled at them. "It's nice to meet you."

"Everyone, this is Audrey."

It made her realize that he didn't even know her last name, so he couldn't give it even if he wanted.

"Nice to meet you, Audrey." The woman he'd introduced as Chris, smiled at her. "Are you guys just here for the weekend?"

"The whole week," said Audrey. "I've never been here before. It's beautiful. Do you live here?"

Chris laughed. "Sort of." She turned to Seymour. "I say I still live here, but this guy sort of lives in LA and Montana, too. So, we spend a lot of time there."

Marianne smiled. "And we're in the same boat. We live here, as much as we can, but Clay needs to be in Nashville a lot of the time, too."

Audrey glanced at Clay and then it hit her. Clay McAdam! He didn't look familiar because he was someone who she'd run into at the grocery store. He was one of the biggest names in country music. He smiled as if he knew that she'd just figured it out.

"I think it's fair to say that we all think of this place as home, though," he added and turned to Ted. "Has the Summer Lake bug bitten you, too? You don't usually stay the whole week."

Ted smiled. "Marcus asked me to stay. I love spending time with them."

"Grandkids," said Chris. "They change your life, don't they?"

Audrey smiled at her but didn't answer. She didn't have any grandchildren yet.

Ted's arm tightened around her. "It's good to see you all, but we should get going."

"It's lovely to meet you," Marianne told Audrey. "I hope we'll see you again."

Out of all of them, Audrey got the idea that Marianne was the only one who'd figured out that she and Ted weren't an established couple.

"Thanks. It's nice to meet you, too."

"Will you guys still be here on Saturday night?" asked Chris.

Audrey looked at Ted. "I think so," he answered.

"Great. You should come out to the Boathouse. Clay's going to sing."

Ted raised an eyebrow at Audrey. She'd planned to leave on Saturday, but she didn't have to. She smiled and he took that as a yes.

"I guess we'll see you there then," he told them.

As they walked back out through the restaurant, Audrey hoped that this wasn't the end of the evening. She wasn't sure that she was ready to take him back to her room with her, but she didn't want to say goodnight yet either.

"Do you want to take another walk around the plaza?" he asked.

"I'd love to." Yet again, it seemed that he'd read her mind.

"I hope it was okay to stop and say hello to them."

She smiled. "It was more than okay, thank you. At least, I know you're not ashamed of me."

He laughed. "That's crazy talk! I was thrilled to get the chance to show you off. They've only ever seen me by myself. I hope you don't mind that I let them think we're here together."

"I kind of like it. It could have been awkward explaining that we only met each other last night. Are they good friends of yours?"

"I suppose they are, now. Chris and Marianne are sisters."

"I thought they might be. They look alike."

"Yes. They both moved up here to be close to their kids. Clay … I'm not sure why he first came here, I don't think he has family here, but he met Marianne and they got together— they're getting married soon."

"Yes. Now I know who he is I remember seeing a story about that. Some of the women at the office were sad that he's finally off the market."

Ted laughed. "Was he on the market before? Like a slab of meat?"

She laughed with him. "No, more like a hunk."

He stopped walking and gave her a mock indignant look. "A hunk, huh? Should I be worried?"

She shook her head. "I won't deny that he's a good-looking man. Seymour is, too, for that matter," she couldn't resist adding.

His eyebrows slid higher.

"But," she reached up and touched his cheek, "Neither of them is the best-looking man around here."

His lips quirked up into a smile—and he proved her point. She hadn't thought that a smile could be kind and sexy at the same time, until she'd met him. He blew out an exaggerated sigh. "Are you going to tell me that there's some other guy you've got your eye on, too?"

She nodded.

"Go on then, who is he?"

She tapped two fingers in the middle of his chest. "The best-looking guy around here, the one I have my eye on—in fact, the one I can't take my eyes off—is you."

He grinned. "Little old me?"

She laughed. "Yes, you. How many times do I have to say it?"

He chuckled. "As many as you like. I'll never get tired of hearing that." He put his hands on her shoulders and looked down into her eyes. "I hope you'll never get tired of hearing me tell you how beautiful you are, either." She got lost in his eyes as he lowered his head until her own eyes closed when he claimed her mouth in a kiss.

She sagged against him and got lost in the way he made her feel. Everything else disappeared; the empty cobbled street around them, and every thought in her head floated away. Only his strong arms around her held her in reality.

When he finally lifted his head, she slowly came back to her senses. He hoped that she'd *never* get tired of hearing him say she was beautiful? It was a nice idea but never was a long time. Much as she was enjoying getting caught up in what was going on between them, she hardly expected it to last.

He cocked his head to one side, looking concerned. "Did I say too much?"

"No. It was a nice thing to say."

"It's a nice thing to hope for, don't you think?"

Her heart raced in her chest. He wasn't backing down from it? "It is, but ..."

"Too soon or too crazy?"

She smiled. "Too soon." She reached up and planted a peck on his lips. "And maybe just a little crazy."

Chapter Ten

Ted pulled his phone out of his back pocket when it rang. "Buenos días," he answered.

Diego laughed. "I almost didn't call."

"Why?"

"Because I thought perhaps you were not taking your walk on the beach this morning."

"I'm here." Ted looked around. Much as he enjoyed his morning walk, he too had wondered whether he might skip it this morning.

"And Audrey?"

He smiled to himself. He knew Diego would want to know everything that had happened since he left. "Audrey's not here."

"Tell me you saw her last night."

"I did."

"But you didn't see her this morning? She didn't stay with you?"

"No."

"Ted!"

He had to laugh. "What?"

"I thought you were going to make the most of this week. She likes you. It's obvious. Why didn't you close the deal?"

"It's not a deal. I'm not looking to close her. I'm getting to know her."

"The fastest way to get to know a woman is in bed."

He had to laugh. "Perhaps in your world. Not in mine."

"So, what are you saying? That this is something more than just a fling?"

"I'd like it to be."

Diego was quiet for a long moment.

"Do you have a problem with that?"

"No. No problem. She seems like a nice person. But have you thought this through?"

"No. I haven't. If you must know, I'm trying not to. Because if I think about it too much, I'll overanalyze it and decide that it's a mistake. I'm trying to do what you tell me to do so often. I'm trying to make the most of every day."

"If you were making the most of every day, you'd still be in bed with her. What you're trying to do is fool yourself about how deep you're in. You've only known her a couple of days."

"I know! And you're the one who thinks I should have already slept with her!"

Diego chuckled. "Okay. I'm not trying to give you a hard time. I was hoping that you were having some fun."

"I am. Just not the kind you were thinking of."

"Okay. Okay. You do as you wish, and I'll be here, keeping my mouth shut."

"I haven't missed the fact that you're keeping your mouth shut about Izzy. What happened when you took her home?"

"Just that. I took her home."

"Home home, or you left her at the airport?"

"Home."

Ted laughed. "Now it's your turn to sound guarded. Want to tell me what happened?"

"Nothing happened. I gave her a ride home. She gave me a drink and then I went back to the airport and continued on my way ... like a good boy."

"And I'm supposed to believe that?"

"You can believe it or not, but it's true."

"And why didn't you *close the deal* as you so eloquently put it?"

"There is no deal to close. I told you. She's quite a woman, but she's not looking for a man. She prefers little boys."

"Are you still stinging over her saying she liked Eddie?"

"No. I'm stinging over the fact that she's dating her boy toy personal trainer!"

"Ah. Sorry."

Diego blew out a sigh. "Don't be. I was stupid. I already told you that she and I would not be a good match, but I let my enthusiasm get the better of me and stuck my neck out."

"And got your face slapped?"

"Not exactly. Just my ego a little dented."

"I'm sorry."

"It's not important. What is important is catching you up on the plan for the day. Will you be available for the team call at noon?"

"Of course."

"Okay. I'll email you my notes by eleven. When do you plan to see Audrey again?"

"Not until tonight."

"You're taking her for dinner?"

"No. Meeting her for a drink afterward. I'm here because Marcus wanted me to stay, remember? I'm having dinner with them."

"So, you're having Audrey as a nightcap?"

"No. I'm having a nightcap with her."

"Don't you want to? Does she not want to?"

Ted closed his eyes for a moment, remembering the way she'd kissed him back when he left her at her door last night. She'd been waiting, willing, for him to come inside, but he'd held back. She hadn't been on a first date in thirty-three years—he didn't want to make her the kind of girl who slept with a guy on the first date.

Diego laughed. "So, do it! You only have a week. Do you want to come home and regret the chances you missed?"

"No." He really didn't. "Let's move on, huh? Tell me how things are looking this morning?"

"Okay."

By the time he hung up fifteen minutes later, the sun had risen above the mountains, and the day was starting to warm up. Ted took off his jacket and slung it over his shoulder. He needed to get going. He was meeting Eddie at the bakery for a late breakfast before the midday conference call.

"Good morning!"

Audrey turned as she was crossing the lobby and smiled at Roxy, who was sitting at the reception desk.

"Good morning, Roxy."

"I hope I didn't overstep last night. I was just so pleased to see Mr. Rawlins going out on a date. I've never known him to do that. And I was thrilled when I realized you were the one he was going with. I hope you had a good time? Damn. Sorry. Forget I even asked!"

Audrey laughed. "It's all right. I don't mind. And yes, we had a lovely time, thank you."

"That's awesome. Are you going to see him again?"

"Yes."

"Sorry! I can't help it."

Audrey had to laugh. "It's all right. You remind me of my daughter, Ally. She's the same way."

"Oh, that's right. You're Ally's mom, aren't you."

"Yes, do you know her?"

"Only through Eddie." Roxy smiled. "When you come to Summer Lake, you discover what a small world it really is. Eddie's one of the gang of people we all hang out with—and of course, he plays in the band at the resort. Ally and Eddie know each other from when she used to sing. And now, you know Eddie's dad. Who knows, maybe you'll both end up moving here and living happily ever after like everyone else!"

"I hardly think so. We've been on one date. And besides, I live in Ventura, and he lives in Laguna Beach."

"Of course. Sorry. But stranger things have happened, you know. Clay McAdam moved here. So did Seymour Davenport."

"That's who he is!"

Roxy gave her a puzzled look.

"We ran into them last night. It took me a minute before I realized that Clay was Clay McAdam. I thought Seymour looked familiar as well, but I couldn't place him."

Roxy winked. "We have our very own pack of silver-foxes here."

Audrey had to laugh. "You can say that again."

"And there's Zack's dad, too."

Audrey frowned. "Oh, Diego?"

"Yes. There's quite a few girls in town who were very disappointed when they saw your friend leaving with him yesterday."

"Well, according to Izzy, they have nothing to worry about."

"No? She doesn't like him?"

Audrey shrugged, suddenly wondering why she was telling Roxy this. "She claims not."

Roxy seemed to sense the change in her and sat back. "So, what does your day hold? Are you sightseeing, shopping or relaxing?"

"First of all, I'm going to go over to the plaza for breakfast, and then I might do a little shopping. I treated myself in Hayes the other day, and I think I might treat myself to another outfit or two while I'm here."

"Oh, you should! Holly has such gorgeous clothes, and she's so clever in helping you find what works for you. I heard that

Roberto's here, too. If you're lucky, you might get both of them at the same time. It's usually pretty quiet in the plaza on a Monday morning."

"I like the sound of that. I'll get going then. You have a good day, Roxy."

"Thanks, and you, too, Ms. Patterson."

"Call me, Audrey."

"Okay. Have a good one, Audrey."

She enjoyed the feel of the sun on her back as she walked over to the plaza. It was going to be a warm day. When she reached the square in front of the clock tower, she glanced over at the café but decided to keep on going and see if Hayes was open yet. She wasn't really hungry, she could get breakfast later, and the thought of having not only Roberto but also Holly Hayes herself to help find her some more outfits was too good to pass up.

The store looked to be open, even though it wasn't ten o'clock yet. The door opened when she pushed it, and she went inside. The first person she saw was neither Roberto nor Holly, but Marianne—one of the women Ted had introduced her to last night.

"Audrey, isn't it?" Marianne greeted her with a smile.

"Yes. It's nice to see you again, Marianne."

"Well, hello, gorgeous!" Roberto came hurrying toward her. "How was your evening? I'll bet you were the belle of the ball. Are you back for more of my magic?"

Audrey smiled. "It was wonderful, thank you."

Roberto winked. "I'll bet *horrible him* was kicking himself when he saw you. That was some way to make a statement about your new beginning, girlfriend!"

Audrey glanced at Marianne, who had politely turned away and was looking at a display of earrings, but who must still be able to hear every word.

Roberto's eyes grew wide, and he mouthed, *Sorry!*

It was hardly his fault. "It was a good evening, thanks. And Richard did seem impressed with the dress." She said it more for Marianne's sake than Roberto's. She didn't want her thinking that she'd been in here talking about Ted as some *horrible him!*

Roberto smiled. "Exes are like that, darling. They're too dumb to know what they have until they lose you. Anyway. That's not why you're here. So, tell me, what can I do for you?"

"Berto, can you come and … oh! I'm sorry." A young woman came out of the dressing room with a tape measure in one hand and a pen and paper in the other. She smiled at Audrey. "I didn't know there was anyone here. I'm Holly, it's nice to meet you."

"You, too. I'm Audrey. And don't worry about me. I'm happy to wait." She nodded at Roberto. "I'm in no hurry, I can browse."

Roberto followed Holly into the dressing room, and Audrey turned to peruse a rack of blouses.

Marianne came to stand beside her. "Sorry about that. My sister, Chris, is back there. They're fitting her wedding dress."

"That's lovely. She must be so excited."

Marianne nodded. "It is. She is." She chuckled. "Well, I think she's more anxious about me and my dress. I still haven't found mine."

"You're her ... bridesmaid? Maid of honor?"

Marianne laughed. "Oh, sorry. I thought you might know. I'm getting married, too."

"Congratulations. When?"

"As soon as I can figure it all out. I don't have a dress. I don't have a date. Clay's been so patient with me, but Chris is starting to stress out over it. I told her all she has to worry about is her own wedding."

"Let me guess; you're sisters, but you're total opposites?"

Marianne nodded. "Yep. She's the organized one. I told her early on that I should probably hire a wedding planner, but she insisted that there's no need. That I can do it myself. She forgets that planning and organizing are not my idea of fun."

Audrey almost suggested that she should get in touch with Ally. She'd been working as a wedding planner for the last couple of years and was about ready to branch out on her own. But it didn't seem appropriate. "Perhaps you should go ahead and hire one?"

"I'm starting to think it's the only way we'll ever get married. Either that or we could elope, but I don't think that would go down too well."

"Probably not, though if I were you, I'd be tempted to do that."

Marianne smiled. "How long have you and Ted known each other?"

Audrey swallowed. She and Ted had deliberately avoided telling his friends that they were on a first date last night—she didn't even know why, but they had. Still, Marianne had seemed as if she knew. "Not long."

"I thought so. Am I right in thinking that when we all assumed you were together, neither of you wanted to say in front of the other that you have no idea where this is going yet because you only just met?"

Audrey chuckled. "That about sums it up."

"I like Ted. You don't have anything to worry about with him. He's …" she thought about it for a moment or two, then smiled. "He's a man of integrity. I know that probably sounds like a strange thing to say, but that's who he is. I think he and Diego had some murky past, but they're above board and well-respected members of the business community these days."

Audrey nodded. She wasn't sure what she could say to that.

"Anyway, sorry." Marianne waved a hand. "Are you just here on vacation, then?"

"Yes. I run an advertising agency, and things have been crazy for the last few months. I came here for the weekend for my children's birthday party, and my assistant, Izzy, talked me into staying here for the week to get a break and decompress."

"Is she here with you?"

"No. She's holding down the fort at work. I say she's my assistant, but she's so much more than that. She could run the place and never miss me."

"Are you here by yourself, then?"

"Yes. Just getting some me-time."

"That's wonderful. A girl needs some of that every now and then. But if you want some company other than your own—or Ted's—we could have lunch, if you like? I'm home alone this week. Clay's going back to Nashville, and Chris and Seymour are heading up to Montana to see his family." She smiled. "You can say no, of course, but if you want to meet up ..."

"I'd love to." She liked Marianne and felt as though the two of them could become friends. It'd been a long time since she'd made any new friends, and this week was supposed to be about new beginnings. "Whatever suits you, whenever suits you. I'm up for it."

"Well, what are you doing when you get finished here?"

"I planned to have a late breakfast at the café. I haven't eaten yet."

"Want to call it an early lunch?"

"That'd be great, and we can go whenever you're ready. I can come back and shop another time."

"No, you're fine. You're here to shop, so shop. And besides, you can't pass up the opportunity of having both Holly and Roberto here. I'm in no hurry to get going anyway."

And shop they did. It was twelve-thirty by the time they emerged from Hayes, each laden down with shopping bags.

Marianne grinned. "Chris won't believe that I bought so much."

"It's a shame she couldn't have stayed, too."

"It is, but this morning was just a quick stop for her before she and Seymour left for Montana. They're due back on Thursday; maybe the three of us can do something."

Audrey nodded. She liked the idea of that. She'd expected this week to be more of a solitary retreat. She'd never have expected that she'd be dating and making new friends.

They found a table out on the terrace of the café, and she sat down with a sigh of relief. "I don't remember the last time I did this much shopping."

Marianne laughed. "Me neither. I'm not much of a shopper, but that was fun."

Audrey watched as Marianne waved at a man who was sitting on the other side of the terrace. He was probably in his mid-forties. Good-looking, rugged—he looked as though he knew how to take care of himself, and probably of anyone around him, too. She was intrigued as to who he might be and how Marianne knew him, but she didn't like to ask.

Marianne caught her expression and smiled. "Don't worry. I'm not making eyes at a younger man while Clay's not around. That's Adam; he's Clay's security guy."

"Oh, I see." She really didn't see. She couldn't imagine what it would be like to date someone as famous as Clay McAdam, and to have a *security guy*—did that just mean bodyguard?—follow you around.

Marianne seemed to know what she was thinking. "It's funny how life changes, the things you get used to that not so long ago would have seemed ridiculous."

"It doesn't seem ridiculous," Audrey said hurriedly.

"I thought it was at first," said Marianne. "Unfortunately, I found out all too soon that it's necessary, too. And Adam's a great guy; so is Davin, his colleague. I just kind of see them as family now." She smiled. "Anyway, tell me about your family?

You said you came here for your children's birthday party. How old are they?"

"Thirty." She blew out a sigh. "It's hard to believe that my babies are thirty. They're twins, Ally and Brayden. What about you, do you have children?"

"I have a daughter, Laura. She has one of the shops here ... the jewelry store."

"Laura Hamilton? She's your daughter? You must be so proud of her. I love her jewelry."

"Thank you. I'm very proud of her. And of her husband, too. Smoke. He's a pilot."

"Do they have children? Are you a grandma?"

"No." Marianne gave her a rueful smile. "They're both so independent and busy with their careers. I do have a little bit of hope. Laura always used to say never when it came to having babies. Lately, she's been saying never say never, and even Smoke is starting to get a little broody. Some of their friends have little ones, and I think they're starting to wonder if it's something they should consider before it's too late. Selfishly, I hope they do. I'd love to have a grandbaby or three, and I think they'd make wonderful parents. But all I can do is wait and hope. What about you?"

"No. My two just had their thirtieth birthday, but neither of them is looking to settle down yet."

"What do they do?"

"Brayden works in cybersecurity. He's always been the techy type. Ally's the outgoing one. She's worked all kinds of jobs over the years, but for the last few, she's been a wedding planner."

Marianne clapped her hands together. "Does she freelance? As you know, I could use her help!"

"I thought that when you first mentioned it, but I didn't want to seem pushy. And besides, I don't know if she could help you anyway. She still works for an outfit in Ventura. She's done a couple of her own weddings, but I don't know if she's ready to travel this far afield yet—or even if the two of you would hit it off. She says that's one of the most important factors. The bride and the planner need to get along."

"Well, if you want to run the idea by her, maybe we can set up a time to talk."

"Thanks. I'll do that."

"I only want something small and simple and local. Clay's fans would love some big deal fancy affair, but that's not who I am, and I'm the one getting married."

"You seem so down to earth. Was it difficult adapting to his kind of life?"

"No. I was worried that it would be, but he's such a wonderful man. He's pretty down to earth himself. It's a pity he's not here this week. I'd love to have you and Ted over for dinner. Maybe next time?"

Audrey laughed. "I don't know that there'll be a next time. Last night was our first date. We're both here visiting for the week, but ..." She shrugged.

"I'm not a betting kind of girl, but I'd put money on there being a next time. You two just seem right together."

Audrey smiled. She felt the same way. There was something right about being with Ted, but she had to remind herself that she was probably just getting carried away. Dating for the first time in over thirty years was fun and exciting, but it was hardly likely to go anywhere. Just because she felt that she and Ted understood each other didn't mean anything. At least nothing more than the fact that they could have a fun week together.

Chapter Eleven

"Mom, Mom, can Ethan come over?"

April frowned. "When?"

"Now."

"Not tonight."

"Aww, but we have math homework that we want to do together."

Eddie pursed his lips. "Because neither of you can manage to figure it out by yourselves? Come on, dude. More like, you want to play video games?"

Marcus shrugged. "Maybe, after we get done with our homework." He shot Ted a sly grin.

"But Grandad's here because you asked him to stay. Ethan can wait until next week. You see him all the time."

Marcus gave Ted a conspiratorial grin. "I bet Grandad wouldn't mind going to see his new girlfriend instead, would you?"

Ted chuckled. "I'm staying out of it. I'm here if you want me; I'll get out of the way if you don't."

"You're not in the way!" Eddie said adamantly.

Ted felt bad. He'd only been joking.

"No, you could never be in the way, Grandad," said Marcus. "I love you being here, but are you really going to tell me that you don't want to see your new girlfriend again?" He grinned. "Remember, when I was little, you promised me you'd never lie to me."

Ted had to laugh. "I would never lie to you. But you're not putting me on the spot like that. I told you once. I'm staying out of it. I'm not going to be your bargaining chip against your parents."

Marcus blew out an exaggerated sigh. "Fair enough." He turned back to April. "So?"

April looked at Eddie and then at Ted.

"Well," said Eddie, "if you don't want to make the most of the time you could have with your grandad ..."

Marcus made a face. "I do. It's just ..."

Ted took pity on the kid. He didn't like seeing the struggle on his face. "It's okay. I get it. I'm here all week. I know you want to see me, but you don't need the rest of your life to stop because of me." He smiled at April and Eddie. "I don't mind if you don't."

Eddie shook his head. "He and Ethan have been waiting for this new game to come out for months. But ..."

"It's fine. I'm here all week. None of us thought that me staying meant that we had to be in each other's pockets the whole time, did we?"

"That's right," agreed Marcus.

"If Ethan comes, I want to see your homework finished, both of you, before there's any video games," said April.

Marcus grinned. "Sure. It won't take us long." He came and wrapped his arm around Ted. "Thanks, Grandad."

Eddie looked at Ted. "You know we don't want you out of the way, right?"

Ted laughed. "Of course, I do. I want to see you guys just as much as I want to see Marcus."

"Almost as much," said Marcus. "You want to see them, but you want to see me just a little bit more."

Ted chuckled. "I told you. I'm not going to be the source of any tension around here."

"Well, what do you think?" asked Eddie. "Do you want to come down to the dock and fish with April and me, while Marcus and Ethan stay cooped up inside playing video games?"

"I'd love to."

Marcus made a face. "That's not fair." He loved to fish with them, but Ted knew this was Eddie's way of making a point.

"Of course, it's fair," said April. "You're the one who gets to choose. You can't have it all ways."

"I know." He was a good kid, just trying to find the balance between wanting to do his own thing with his friends and wanting to spend time with the men in his life. He looked at Ted. "You're going to come back tomorrow, right? And every night this week?"

"Maybe not every night," said Eddie.

"But, we can go fishing before you leave?"

"Of course, we can."

Once Ethan arrived, he and Marcus disappeared into the bedroom, and Ethan's mom, Megan, stood chatting with April. Eddie looked at Ted. "Want to head down to the dock?"

Ted loved sitting out here with Eddie. It was an old wooden dock that reminded him of where he used to take Eddie as a kid. It made him happy that Eddie loved this place so much. It was a nice property, down on the water, but nothing fancy. Eddie could buy any of the bigger houses in town; he could have a grander place and a much nicer dock if he wanted, but he chose not to. He said that for April and him, the priority was to have a place where they were comfortable, a place that felt like home. They didn't need fancy.

Eddie cast his line and then sat down beside Ted and offered him a beer from the cooler.

"Thanks. Is April coming down?"

"Probably not. She'll no doubt chat with Megan for a while, but she planned to do some studying tonight anyway. She was going to leave the three of us to have a boys' night. Do you mind that Marcus is hanging with Ethan instead?"

"Of course not. I'm not here to demand that he spend every spare minute with me. I just like being around to be part of your everyday lives. And him having his friend over is his everyday life."

Eddie nodded. "I guess. I just ... don't take this the wrong way, but I would have given anything to have you there wanting to spend the evening with me after school when I was his age."

Ted's heart clenched in his chest. "I'm sorry, son."

"Don't be! I didn't mean it that way. It was Mom who did that to us, not you."

"I should never have listened to her."

"Neither should I."

"You were just a little kid. I should have known better. I should have fought to be able to stay in your life."

"And you would have if you thought I wanted you in it, right?" Eddie took a slug of his beer. "Let's drop it, can we? I only get mad at her when I think about it. And all's well that ends well, we have each other now."

Ted knew he should be grateful for that, but he couldn't help resenting Irene—and himself—for all the years he'd lost.

"Anyway," said Eddie, "I'm kind of glad it's worked out this way. I want to hear about Ally's mom." He smiled. "Your new girlfriend."

Ted smiled through pursed lips. "I'd hardly call her that."

"Yet?"

He met Eddie's gaze. "I don't know. She's … I … I don't know what to say, son. I met her on Saturday night, it's only Monday now."

"Yeah, but you like her, don't you?"

"I do. I'm not going to lie to you. A part of me is very interested to see what might happen between us."

"And the rest of you?"

"The rest of me thinks I'm a fool. I'm too old. I don't need a woman in my life. I have you and April and Marcus. I have work, and of course, there's Diego. Why would I look for something more?"

"Because I think deep down, we all want someone to love, someone to share life with. I have no idea if Audrey might be that someone for you, but she could be. You won't know if you don't explore it."

Ted nodded and stared out at the lake. He'd believed that he didn't need someone to share his life with. The one time he'd tried, it hadn't ended well. It had cost him his relationship with his son. He hadn't ever wanted to give anyone that much power over his life and his happiness again.

"When are you seeing her again?"

Ted tried to hide his smile, but he couldn't.

"Tonight?" asked Eddie.

"Yes."

"So, why the hell are you sitting here with me?"

"Because there's nowhere else on earth I'd rather be. I missed way too many years of your life, son. I'm hardly going to pass up an opportunity like this. Audrey and I plan to meet later. I'm looking forward to seeing her, but it's not more important than this."

Eddie held up his bottle, and Ted chinked his against it. "I get the feeling that the day will come when you bring her here with you, and she'll be a part of this—not something that you have to choose instead of this."

Ted took a slug of his beer. He liked the sound of that, but he knew it was too soon to even think about it.

~ ~ ~

Audrey checked herself over in the mirror and smiled. Roberto had done her proud again. He and Holly had put together a whole new wardrobe for her this morning. It had been so much fun shopping with them and hanging out with Marianne. It'd felt like she really was starting a new chapter in her life. New clothes, new friends, a new place—which she was already starting to love—and a new man. Well, she could hardly call him that, but still. She applied a little lipstick and pressed her lips together. She was aware of the lines around her mouth, and her eyes, too. But she didn't mind them. Some of the women she knew, especially in the advertising world, fought hard to stave off any sign of aging. She didn't feel the need. She'd earned every line—and she fought every pound! She lost more of those than fights than she'd like, but she stayed in some kind of shape. She chuckled. At least, it was a shape other than round.

She glanced at the clock on the bedside table. It was only eight. She'd ordered room service for dinner earlier, preferring to eat before she got changed for her date with Ted. She wanted to look good in her new clothes, and she had a terrible habit of managing to spill whenever she wore something new. She used to joke that she looked good in everything she ate. Her smile faded. She used to feel so comfortable in that life— her old life with Richard. Maybe she'd gotten too comfortable. Who could blame him for falling for the young and immaculate Natalee when his wife was a slob who had let herself go so far that she even joked about it?

No. She picked up her wineglass and took a sip. She wasn't going to go blaming herself. She wasn't going to exempt herself from all blame, but she was hardly responsible for Richard's choice to lie and cheat.

The only constructive thing she could do with that line of thought was to take the lessons she'd learned about becoming too complacent in a relationship and apply them to her new life. She didn't know if she and Ted would embark on a relationship, so she couldn't say she would apply the lessons there, but she did know that she wanted to see herself as an attractive woman—because if she didn't see herself that way, why would he?

She jumped when her phone buzzed with a text and smiled when she saw Ted's name on the display.

I should be back over there by eight-thirty if you want to get together then?

The butterflies took to flight in her stomach once again.

Great. Shall I meet you in the lobby?

There was a bar in the restaurant; she assumed that they'd go there. She doubted that the café over in the plaza would be open much longer.

His reply set her heart racing.

I can come to you if you like?

"Oh. I'd like!" She told her phone. "But the last two nights, you've left me all hot and bothered on my doorstep." She chuckled. She wanted to tell him that he should only come here if he understood that she might not let him leave again. That was probably a little too forward, though, even for the new, upfront and honest Audrey.

Great. You can come whenever you're ready.

She tapped out the message quickly, hoping that he wouldn't wonder why she'd hesitated before she replied. She read it over and hit send with a smile, hoping that he wouldn't read into it the same double entendre that she just had.

See you soon.

She looked around the room, it was neat and tidy, she had no concerns there. They could sit out on the balcony; it was still pleasant out there. If it got cooler, they could come inside. She let out a little laugh, she needed to calm her nerves—or her excitement, she wasn't sure which was making her so giddy. The thought of him coming inside! A shiver ran down her spine. She hadn't had sex in … way too long. She really didn't want to do the math and know for certain just how long it'd been. She'd rather focus on the number she did know—the one that set her body tingling. Thirty-three years. That was how long it had been since she'd had sex with someone who wasn't Richard. She'd dated some back then and had had some fun. Now, more than half a lifetime later, she was ready to have some more.

She went back into the bathroom and sprayed her wrist with perfume, which she then rubbed into her neck. With a smile, she pressed her wrist between her breasts, wondering if the way tonight went would mean that Ted got to smell it there.

A jolt of excitement shot through her when she heard the knock on the door. She started to hurry toward it and then stopped and took a deep breath. She held her hands out in front of her and was pleased to see that they were only shaking slightly. She opened the door and sucked in a deep breath when she saw him.

He was so incredibly handsome! He looked as though he'd stepped out of a magazine. His gray hair was perfect, his eyes shone as he smiled at her—and boy, that smile!

"Hi!" He pulled his hand out from behind his back to present her with a bunch of flowers—roses of every color imaginable.

"Oh, my goodness! Thank you!"

"I don't know what flowers you like; I don't even know if you like them. You're not allergic, are you?"

She shook her head with a laugh. "No. I'm not. These are beautiful, thank you. Roses are my favorites, and I can never decide which color I like best, so these are perfect. You couldn't have chosen better if you did know. Come on in."

She led him inside and looked around, wondering what she could use as a vase to put them in.

"I thought about that," said Ted. "Check the cabinet next to the fridge. I found a spare carafe for the coffee pot in mine. If you don't have one, we can go and get that."

Audrey checked and wasn't surprised to see that there wasn't a spare carafe there. Her coffee maker used pods.

"Do you want to come with me?" asked Ted.

She had to bite back a laugh. Her mind was still caught up in thoughts of going to bed with him. "Of course," she answered, glad that he wasn't aware which question she was really answering.

When they got to his room, he stopped outside the door. "I think it's tidy in there, but forgive me if it's not?"

She laughed. "I can wait outside if you prefer."

"No." He took her hand and led her inside.

She wasn't surprised to see that it was indeed tidy. He didn't strike her as someone who left things out of place.

He went to the cabinet and pulled out the spare carafe. "We can go and get a vase for them tomorrow, but this should get them through the night."

She nodded and had to swallow as a wave of desire coursed through her. She wasn't sure what did it, perhaps the thought of him getting her through the night. She'd kept having little fantasies about sleeping with him, but not about *sleeping* with him. What would it be like to wake up beside him? And was she about to find out?

It seemed that whatever it was, it affected him, too. He set the carafe down on the counter and came toward her. He put his hands on her shoulders and looked down into her eyes. "I've been thinking about you all day."

"I've been thinking about you, too." She slid her arms up around his neck and stepped closer as he circled his arms around her waist.

"I want to take this slowly, Audrey. There's no rush."

She held his gaze, hoping that her eyes could tell him what her mouth didn't want to say. He lowered his head and claimed her mouth in a kiss that belied his words. His hands roved over her, up and down her back, one tangling in her hair, the other closing around her ass and holding her against him as he rocked his hips.

She clung to him in a desperate effort to stay upright. She wasn't equipped to deal with the effect he had on her. Her knees felt like jelly.

He lifted his head and looked down at her. His breath was coming slow and shallow. "We should wait."

"Why?" She was surprised at the way it sounded; it was a desperate plea. She didn't want to wait. She wanted him to take her, right here right now, and that one moaned syllable made that abundantly clear.

He looked as though he was in pain as he shook his head. "It's too soon. I don't want this to be just a quick … a quick … one and done."

"Neither do I … it doesn't have to be." She felt a smile spread across her face as a thought occurred to her. "But the sooner we get started, the more chances we'll have—and the better we'll get."

He laughed. "You're going to try to persuade me?"

She nodded, shocked at herself, but not about to back down. "Apparently, I have no shame."

He cupped her face between his hands. "There's nothing shameful about it. It's … damn, it's a turn-on. I'm not going to make you ask twice. I need you to know; I want you." He ran his hands down her sides, and she felt herself tremble under his touch.

She lifted her lips, and he claimed her mouth again in a kiss that left her with no doubt that he wanted her just as much as she wanted him.

Chapter Twelve

Ted forced himself to take his time. He hadn't stopped thinking about this moment since he'd left her outside her door on Saturday night. It'd taken everything he had to walk away from her then, and even more to walk away again last night. He'd used up every last reserve of willpower he had.

He let his hands rove over her as he kissed her, trying to get some feel for how she would respond. She was eager if he went by her words, but he knew she might be more hesitant when it came down to it. The last thing he wanted to do was rush into something she wasn't ready for.

He needn't have worried. Her hands roved over his chest, and she started to unfasten the buttons on his shirt. That only heightened his desire for her. He slid his hands under her skirt and closed them around her ass. That did nothing for his attempt to take it slowly. Her ass was full and round, and her skin was soft and warm. He needed to feel more of it against him.

He got rid of the skirt and then unfastened the buttons on her blouse as she watched. She was breathing deeply, and the rise and fall of her breasts mesmerized him. When the blouse was gone, he unfastened her bra and filled his hands with her full breasts. She gave a little moan that reminded him that he needed to get rid of his pants. He stepped back and let his gaze wander over her.

Her hands came up and covered her breasts. "They don't get out much," she said with an embarrassed laugh.

He took hold of her hands and gently moved them away. "Don't. Please. I want to see you. You're beautiful." He ducked his head, trailed his tongue over each nipple in turn. They tightened into stiff little buds that only made him stiffer.

He led her to the bed and sat her down while he quickly got rid of his pants. She held her arms up to him, and he sat beside her, then pulled her down to lie with him.

"Are you okay?"

She nodded. "I think so."

He cupped her breast in his hand, then trailed it over her stomach and on down between her legs, holding her gaze the whole while. She turned her head and looked away when he touched her.

"Look at me."

She did, and he dropped a kiss on her lips. "I want to do this with you, not to you."

She frowned.

"I don't want you to look away; I don't want you to feel embarrassed. I want you to enjoy me, let me enjoy you. Don't hide inside your head. Stay here with me … let's figure it out together."

She searched his face and then nodded. He traced her opening with his fingertip, and she bit down on her bottom lip.

"Does that feel good?"

She nodded.

He circled her with his thumb and pressed his finger a little deeper.

"So good," she breathed.

To his surprise, her fingers closed around him and began to move up and down his length. "Does that?"

He closed his eyes and enjoyed it for a moment. "Maybe a little too good." He moved out of her reach and curled his arm around her, pulling her closer. "I want you, Audrey."

She smiled. "So, what are you waiting for?"

He lowered his head and claimed her mouth, kissing her deeply, while he made sure she was ready. He rolled her nipple between his finger and thumb until she writhed underneath him, then he slid his hand back between her legs. She was hot and wet, and when he circled her with his thumb again, she gasped and rocked her hips.

"Please," she breathed.

He positioned himself above her, spreading her legs with his knees.

Her arms came up around his shoulders, and when she said it again, "Please, Ted," he had no choice but to give her what she wanted.

He thrust his hips and gasped as he sank into her velvety wetness. Her fingers dug into his back, and her legs came up and wrapped around his. All restraint was gone. He thrust his hips in a desperate rhythm, needing to be deeper and deeper inside her. She moved with him, matching every thrust, her head thrown back, all caution gone.

He pushed himself up on his hands so he could go deeper and harder. She looked up into his eyes and moaned as she moved with him. "Yes," she gasped, and he felt her start to tense. "Oh, God! Ted! Yes!" She let herself go as her orgasm took her, and her inner muscles clenched around him, gripping him tighter and tighter until he surrendered to her. The tension that had built inside him found its release in a great wave of pleasure that made him see stars as he came hard. Their bodies melded into one as they carried each other away.

When they finally lay still, he looked down into her eyes.

"Wow!" she murmured.

"I—" Ted clamped his jaw shut just in time. He had no idea where those three words had come from, and even if they felt true, he knew he couldn't say them yet—for her sake or for his. "I think you're amazing, Audrey." It sounded trite, but even that was preferable to telling her that he loved her! He wasn't a kid who was so overwhelmed with the rush of lovemaking that he should mistake it for the real thing.

She smiled. "I think you're pretty great yourself."

He rolled to the side and wrapped his arms around her, dropping a kiss in her hair. "You were right."

"About what?"

He smiled. "You said that the sooner we made love, the more chances we'd have to do it again—if you want to?"

She rolled onto her side and looked into his eyes. "Oh, I want to."

"Good." He dropped a kiss on the tip of her nose. "Because I do."

~ ~ ~

When Audrey opened her eyes, it took her a moment to figure out where she was—and why there was a weight on her stomach. She was in Ted's bed, in his hotel room, and he had his arm around her, holding her to his chest. She closed her eyes again with a smile and nestled against him. She'd wondered what it might be like to wake up beside him, and now she knew; it felt good.

A wave of warmth rushed through her as she remembered last night. After he'd made love to her, they'd sat out on the balcony in robes and had a glass of wine as they watched the stars come out over the lake. When it had gotten too cold, they'd come back inside, and he'd warmed her up in the nicest possible way. Warm was too tame a word; it had been hot! A shiver ran down her spine as she remembered the way it had felt when they'd made love a second time.

His arm tightened around her waist, and she turned to look over her shoulder. He was awake and smiling.

"Good morning, beautiful."

"Good morning."

She turned over, and he landed a kiss on her lips.

"Did you get any sleep?"

She smiled. "You wore me out; I slept like a log. I didn't snore or do anything embarrassing, did I?"

He laughed. "Not that I heard, though I slept well."

She pulled herself up to a sitting position and pulled the sheet up with her to cover her breasts. She needed to go to the bathroom, but she was buck naked and didn't relish the thought of parading her bare ass in front of him.

"Do you want coffee?"

She nodded vigorously. "You have no idea how much."

He got up and turned his back to her to pull his boxers on. She wasn't sure if he did it deliberately, but she took advantage to grab her clothes and make her break for the bathroom while he made the coffee.

Before she came back out, she looked at herself in the mirror. She looked different. Her cheeks were flushed, her hair was a mess, but her eyes shone brightly, she looked ... alive. She smiled. She knew what Izzy would say, she looked like she'd got some! And she had.

Ted handed her a mug of coffee when she came out, and she took it with a grateful smile. He was wearing a robe and looked surprised that she was dressed already.

"I thought we could take these outside."

She felt silly. Of course, she could have grabbed a robe instead of getting dressed. She felt as though she'd spoiled things.

"Are you okay?" he asked once they were sitting out on the balcony.

She smiled at him. "I'm fine. Honestly, I feel like I'm screwing this up. I'm not uncomfortable with you, but I don't know what the protocol is here. I got dressed, but I don't want you to think that means I'm ready to leave, I just ..." She shrugged and gave him an apologetic smile.

He set his coffee down and came and squatted down in front of her. He took hold of her hands and smiled up at her. "If there is a protocol, I don't know what it might be either. All I know is that I'm glad you don't want to leave yet. I don't want you to. Do you have any plans for today?"

She smiled, grateful that he was so understanding. "Only vague ones to maybe take a hike, maybe take a drive. Definitely take a shower and have some breakfast."

"Do you want to do any of those things with me? All of them?" he added with a wink.

She nodded. "I'd love to. Maybe not the shower, not today." She liked the idea of showering with him, but not yet. "But the rest of it, yes."

He checked his watch.

"Do you have any plans?" she asked.

"Sorry. It's just that Diego calls at seven."

She smiled. "So how about after our coffee. I'll go back and take a shower and you can talk to Diego and then we'll meet up later?"

He squeezed her hand. "Sounds like a plan to me. I won't be too long. We speak every morning to check in and make sure that the day is on track."

"How about you call me at eight, and we'll see where we're up to?"

"Okay."

After Ted spoke with Diego, he took a shower and paced his room for a while. He wanted to wait until eight before he called her. He wanted to give her some time to herself if she needed it. He checked his watch. It was ten before eight now. He looked at the flowers on the table and smiled. It was thanks to them that she'd come in here last night, and he couldn't be happier that she hadn't left until this morning.

He picked up the carafe. He'd have to find somewhere to buy a vase for them today, but for now, he was going to take them to her. He didn't imagine that she'd mind him showing up at her door again instead of calling.

When he got there, he knocked and then held up the flowers in front of him, hoping to make her smile. Instead, he got a very different reaction when she opened the door.

"Oh. Thank you. Erm. Come in. But I have to go."

He followed her into the room with a frown. "You have to go where? Why?"

She was wringing her hands together, and her bag lay on the bed half packed. "I have to go home. It's Brayden. There's been an accident."

"Oh, no. Is he all right?"

"Yes. No. I don't know. Ally called. She's on the way to the hospital. He was knocked off his bicycle. He cycles to work. All she knows is that he's in the hospital. His coworker called her."

Ted's mind raced. He knew that she and Izzy had flown up here on a commercial flight and driven up from the airport in a rental car. He pulled his phone out of his pocket and called Diego.

"I didn't expect to hear from you again today," Diego answered with a laugh.

"Where's the plane?"

"It's here. Why? What do you need?" The immediate change in Diego's attitude reminded Ted of their earlier days, and just how much he knew he could rely on his old friend.

"Audrey needs to get home in a hurry. Is Zack here?"

"No. He's in Nashville. Let me call Smoke and see if any of his charter planes are available. How many passengers and when?"

"Two." Ted didn't stop to question whether he should go with her. He looked at Audrey, who was watching him with a bewildered expression. "How long do you need to get ready?"

She looked at her bag and then back at him. "I'll be leaving in fifteen minutes."

It was only when she said that that he realized he hadn't asked her if she needed help—or offered any. "Two passengers," he repeated to Diego. "And we can be at the airport within half an hour."

"Okay. Do what you need to, and I'll call you back."

"Thanks." Ted hung up. "Diego's going to find someone to fly us back to Ventura."

She stopped packing and straightened up. "I ... I was going to drive. I ..."

He went to her and put an arm around her shoulders. "You have a rental car. It'll take you a couple of hours to get to the airport, and you don't have a reservation."

She looked at her phone that was sitting on the bedside table. "I'm on hold. Trying to change my ticket."

"Diego knows the guy who runs a charter operation here. He's calling him now. All we need to do is get to Summer Lake airport."

She frowned. He'd guess that she was in shock.

"What can I do?" he asked.

She shook her head. "I don't know. I don't know what I can do. I'm packing my bag." She looked around. "I'm leaving."

He hugged her into his side. "It's going to be okay. It'll take less than an hour, once we get in the air. I'll call ahead and get a rental car for when we land."

"We?"

It hadn't occurred to him until that moment that she might not want him to go with her. "Unless you don't want me to come?"

She blew out a shaky sigh and rested her head against his shoulder. "Thank you."

His phone rang when they were halfway to the Summer Lake airport. "Diego. Talk to me."

"Smoke will take you himself. He's standing by now. How long will it take you?"

"We'll be there in ten minutes."

"Okay. I'll let him know."

Audrey watched him hang up the phone. She felt as though she'd floated through the last half hour. She looked at the clock on the dashboard. It was only half an hour since she'd hung up with Ally. At that point, she'd gone onto automatic pilot. Packing her bag, calling the airline, waiting on hold in the hope that they'd be able to find her a flight. Then Ted had come in and taken over.

He glanced over at her. "Smoke Hamilton is going to take us. He'll have the plane ready when we get there."

"Smoke?"

He nodded. "He owns a couple of planes and runs a charter operation."

"He's Laura's husband?"

"That's right."

She had to pull herself together. Her phone rang, making her jump. It was Ally.

"Hi, sweetheart. What do you know?"

"Not a lot. I came to the hospital. He was unconscious when they brought him in. His leg's broken and … I don't know what else. Are you going to be able to get home?"

"Yes. I'm on the way. I'll be there in a couple of hours."

"How? It takes that long to get to the airport."

"Ted's bringing me. We're going to fly from here."

"Oh. That's good."

"Have you called Izzy?"

"No. Have you?"

"No, but I will. I'll ask her to come and be with you. You shouldn't be there by yourself."

"I'm fine, Mom."

"I'll call her anyway. Have you called your father?"

"No."

Audrey blew out a sigh. "You should."

"I don't want to. If you want him to know, you can tell him."

"Ally!"

"Sorry, Mom. But I don't want to have to deal with him."

"Okay. I'll call him. But I'll call Izzy first; she can come and be with you till I get there."

"Thanks. She'll keep Dad at bay—if he bothers to show up."

"Call me if they tell you anything. That's all they've said so far—that he had a broken leg, and he was unconscious?"

"Yes. They said they'd be able to tell me more after the doctor's been in with him."

"Okay. I'll call Izzy now. I love you."

"Love you, too, Mom. Tell Ted I said thanks for bringing you back?"

"I will."

Audrey hung up and looked at Ted. "His leg is broken, and he was unconscious when they brought him in."

"I'm sure he's going to be fine."

Somehow, when Ted said it, she believed him. It calmed her a little. "I need to call Izzy."

"Go ahead."

Izzy answered on the second ring. "Good morning. Do you have anything exciting to tell me?"

"I have something to tell you, but not what you're expecting. Brayden's in the hospital. Ally's there with him. I'm on the way home. Can you go and stay with her till I get there?"

"Oh, God, Audrey! What happened?"

"He was knocked off his bicycle. He was unconscious, and his leg is broken. That's all I know."

"I'm on my way out the door. Is he at Memorial?"

"Yes."

"Are you on the road? Have you managed to get a flight?"

"Ted's bringing me. We're flying, he says it won't take more than an hour."

"Oh. That's good. And what about Richard?"

"I'm going to call him next."

"Do you want me to do it?"

Audrey thought about it. She wasn't looking forward to making the call, but she knew she should be the one to do it. "Thanks, but no. If he gets there before I do, would you mind keeping the peace? Ally didn't want to call him."

"Sure. Don't worry about it. I can't stand him, but I can be civil to him in these circumstances."

"Thanks, Izzy. I'm going to have to go. We're at the airport."

"Do you need me to pick you up when you land?"

"Thanks, but Ted booked a rental car."

"Well, isn't he turning out to be a hero?"

Audrey glanced over at him as he parked the car in front of the airport building. "Yes. He really is."

"I'm glad. I guess I'll see you at the hospital, then. Call me if I can do anything."

"Okay, and call me if the doctors tell you anything."

Ted got out and came around to open her door. "I'll take your bag and go and talk to Smoke if you like, while you call Richard."

She made a face. "Thanks. I'll be quick. I want to get going."

She watched him walk inside and shake hands with a tall guy who was standing just inside the doors. She took a deep breath and dialed Richard's number.

"Audrey. This is a nice surprise. How are you? I have to tell you, you looked amazing this weekend. I was thinking, it's been too long since we caught up. Do you want to have dinner with me when you get back?"

That was so unexpected, she couldn't even speak for a minute.

"Are you there?"

"Yes. Sorry. Listen, Richard. I'm not calling to chat. I ... it's Brayden."

"What about him?"

"He had an accident this morning. He's in the hospital. Ally's with him. His leg is broken, and he was unconscious when they brought him in."

"Oh, and let me guess, you're off at the lake with Ted Rawlins, so you want me to deal with it?"

She closed her eyes against the sting of his words. She wondered if he'd always been that heartless—had she not noticed until the final years of their marriage, or had he gotten meaner since then? "Actually, Ted and I are on the way there now. I was calling because I thought you might care about our son. I should have known better." She hit the end call button.

Her phone rang again immediately and much as she didn't want to, she answered it.

"I'm sorry, sweetie. I was shocked, and I have to tell you, I'm a little jealous. Of course, I care. Where is he? Is he at Memorial?"

"Yes."

"Okay. And Ally's already there?"

"Yes. And Izzy."

He didn't reply to that.

"Don't worry about it, Richard. I'll let you know how he is."

"Don't hang up on me again, Audrey. We need to talk."

"I don't have time. I'm about to get on the plane."

"Oh, that's right. I forgot. You and Izzy travel by private jet these days. Do you really think a man like Ted Rawlins is going to be interested in you for long? A man with that kind of money can have any woman he wants."

She hit the end call button again. She didn't need that.

Ted stuck his head back out the doors, and she hurried toward him.

"What is it?" he asked when she reached him.

She gave him a puzzled look, and he reached up and wiped away tears she hadn't known were falling.

She shook her head. "Richard." She didn't want to have to explain anything else.

Fortunately, Ted didn't expect her to. A look of anger crossed his face, but he hid it quickly and wrapped her in a hug. Then he took hold of her hand. "Smoke's ready to go."

Smoke led them out across the tarmac. Under any other circumstances, Audrey would have been impressed by both him and the plane. She registered that Izzy would no doubt love him. But she was more concerned with how quickly he could get them to Ventura and to her son.

As the plane thundered down the runway, Ted took hold of her hand and squeezed it. "It won't be long now."

She met his gaze, and fresh tears filled her eyes.

He looked worried. "What did Richard say to you?"

She shook her head. "It's not that. I'm not crying because of him. I have no more tears left for that man." She managed a smile. "You're the one who made me cry—good tears. You've been amazing. Thank you."

He squeezed her hand again. "I'm glad I can help."

Chapter Thirteen

Ted slid behind the wheel of the rental car and blew out a sigh. He'd gotten Audrey here to the hospital. And now she was with Izzy and Ally. To his relief, there'd been no sign of Richard. He had a low-grade anger simmering toward that man. He didn't know what he'd said to Audrey when she spoke to him on the phone before they left the lake, but he did know that whatever it was, it had upset her.

It was only when he'd seen Audrey wrapped up in a hug with Ally and Izzy that he'd questioned himself—did he have any right to be here? He hadn't questioned a thing while he'd been making sure that he could get her to her son as quickly as possible, but now that task had been achieved, he was feeling less sure of himself. He'd stepped in and taken charge without a second thought. Of course, Audrey hadn't minded; she'd been reeling from the news, but he was questioning himself now.

He'd excused himself and come out here to the parking lot. He didn't want to be in the way. He didn't want her to have to factor him into her thinking. She needed to be free to worry about her son and find comfort in her friend and her daughter.

He leaned his head back against the headrest and blew out a sigh at the sunroof.

His phone rang in his pocket, and he almost ignored it. It was no doubt Diego, wondering if there was any news. He pulled it out and checked the screen and was glad he had when he saw Audrey's name.

"Hey," he answered.

"Where are you?"

"I'm just outside, in the parking lot. I thought I should leave you—Are you okay?"

She made a little snuffling sound. "Yes. Of course. I'm fine. Thank you so much. And don't feel you need to wait if … You've done so much already. I don't want you to feel—"

"Audrey?" He could hear the change in her. She was putting distance between them, speaking politely, treating him like a kind stranger. If that was what she wanted, then he'd respect it, but he didn't think it was. She was trying not to be a burden to him, and he needed her to know that she could.

"Yes?"

"Please don't."

"Don't what?"

"Don't change a thing between you and me. I'm here with you … I'm here *for* you because I want to be. I know we haven't known each other very long, but there's something special between us. I know you feel it, too, or I wouldn't say this. Don't try to push me away because you think this is too much for me. It isn't. Okay?"

"Oh, Ted." He could hear the tears and the gratitude in her voice

He had to swallow before he spoke again. "I'll come back in there if you want me there, and I'll wait out here to give you time with your girls—whichever is best for you. Just know this; I'm not going anywhere."

"You're something special, Ted."

"So are you."

"Do you want to come back in here and give me a hug? That's what I'd like the most right now."

He smiled, relieved; it had been a gamble to say all that, it might have been too much to put on her in such a stressful time, but it'd been what she needed to hear—and what he needed to say. "I'm on my way."

When he got back to the waiting room where he'd left them, they were all smiling. Audrey came to him and he circled his arms around her waist, and she rested her head against his shoulder.

"The doctor came out and told us that he's awake. It seems that it's just a concussion. He took a nasty knock to his head, and they're going to set his leg in a cast, but," she blew out a big sigh, "it's not nearly as bad as we thought it might be."

He hugged her tighter. "That's wonderful news. Can you see him?"

"They said maybe in half an hour."

Ally and Izzy came to join them.

Izzy smiled warmly at him. "Aren't you the man of the hour? Thanks for getting her back here so quickly."

Ally reached up and pecked his cheek. "Thanks, Ted. You're awesome."

He tightened his arm around Audrey, who was standing by his side. "I just did what needed to be done."

Izzy smiled. "Diego said you're too modest; he was right."

Audrey's phone rang, and she took it out and frowned.

"Is that Dad?" asked Ally. "You always get that look when it's him."

"It is. I should tell him that he doesn't need to worry."

"He doesn't seem too worried to me," said Izzy. "You got back here from Summer Lake before he's even bothered to call to check on things—and he's only fifteen miles down the road."

Audrey pursed her lips. "I know. And after what he said to me earlier, I'm done with his crap. I'm tired of making excuses for him."

Ted watched her as she answered the call and turned away from them.

"Wow!" said Izzy. "What did he say to her earlier that's got her so pissed?"

"I don't know. She spoke to him before we got on the plane. He upset her somehow. She said it didn't matter, but she was hurt." He glanced at Ally. "I'm sorry. It's not my place to—"

Ally gave him a grim smile. "Don't you dare apologize. We all know he's an asshole; you're just not in a position where you can admit that you know it, too. I hope he doesn't come. Seeing you and Mom together rattled him at the weekend. I think seeing you here will only set him off."

"I should stay out of the way, then."

"No, he should!" Ally and Izzy both spoke at the same time and then smiled at each other.

"See, it's a unanimous decision," said Izzy.

Audrey came back and looked around at them. "Is everything okay?"

"Yep," said Ally. "What about you. Is he coming?"

Audrey shook her head.

"Asshole," muttered Izzy.

"He is," agreed Audrey. "But it works out for the best. I don't want to see him, and I know neither of you do. Brayden won't mind either way and …" She stopped talking as a doctor approached.

"Mrs. Patterson."

"Yes."

"Do you want to come in and see him?"

Audrey nodded and followed her, and Ally scurried after them.

Izzy raised her eyebrows at Ted. "Are you itching to get out of here?"

He shook his head with a smile. He'd expected her to test him out as soon as Audrey wasn't around. "Nope. I'm here for the duration."

She looked skeptical. "Of what? Until Brayden's okay? Until the novelty wears off?"

"I probably shouldn't admit this to you. I haven't told Audrey this yet, and I've only just figured it out for myself."

"What?"

"I'll be around Audrey for as long as she wants me."

Izzy's expression softened, and she reached out and touched his arm. "Aww. You're perfect. You're the real deal, aren't you?"

He chuckled. "Real? Yes. Perfect? Not by a long shot. But my heart's in the right place."

"And your heart's already involved in this, isn't it?"

He held her gaze for a moment and then nodded.

~ ~ ~

Audrey parked the rental car in the driveway and turned to look at Ted. "I feel as though this should seem strange, but it doesn't."

"What should?"

"Having you here, bringing you into my home."

"It doesn't seem strange to me. I wish it were under different circumstances, but I hoped that I'd visit you here soon anyway."

"You did?"

He smiled. "Of course, I did. That's how a relationship works, isn't it? I come to your house, you come to mine."

Her heart was racing. "A relationship?"

He smiled. "That's what I'd like."

"Wow!" She pushed her hair back off her shoulders.

"It's probably not the best time to bring it up—"

"No! It's a wonderful time." She smiled. "It's perfect. Come on, let's go inside. This isn't a conversation we need to have sitting out here in the car."

As he followed her into the house, she wondered how it would look through his eyes. She considered herself very fortunate. The divorce hadn't exactly left her destitute, but her current financial situation was a product of her own hard work since then. Her home was beautiful by anyone's standards. At least, anyone she knew. But before she'd met Ted, she hadn't known anyone who flew around in a private jet.

She led him through to the kitchen. "Would you like a drink?"

"Just water, thanks. This is a beautiful place."

"Thanks, I like it."

"I do, too. Everything about it says Audrey."

She smiled. "Good. That was my plan when I bought it, I wanted to put my own stamp on it."

"Well, you did."

She poured two glasses of iced water and led him through to the den. "I can't thank you enough. If it weren't for you, I'd still be at the airport, trying to get a flight back here."

"I'm glad I was able to help."

She frowned. "What about you, though? You're supposed to be spending time with your family."

"I can do that any time. This was an emergency."

"I thought it was, but it turned out not to be as bad as I feared." She shuddered. It was only now that she knew that Brayden was going to be fine, that she could allow herself to acknowledge all the fears that raced through her mind on the way back here.

"And that's the best possible outcome."

"It is." Her mind was only just starting to catch up with the practical realities of the situation. "Is Smoke still waiting to take you back?"

Ted nodded. "He said he'd stand by until this evening. I didn't know … I didn't know how long you'd need me … or even if you'd want me."

She edged closer to him and put her arms around his neck. "I want to say that I didn't need you, but that would be a lie. I needed your help today, and I'll be forever grateful for it. I do want you …" She hesitated, but only for a moment. He'd stuck his neck out talking about a relationship, she needed him to know that she'd like that, too. "What you said about a relationship? I'd like that. I don't know what it would look like, but I'd like to find out."

He visibly relaxed as he smiled. "It can look however we want it to. We can make it up as we go along."

"We can, but there are some things we can't control."

He frowned. "Like what?"

"Well, for starters, you're supposed to be in Summer Lake visiting your family. I need to be here and at the hospital with Brayden much of the time."

"Absolutely. I understand that. But I'm only at the lake this week, and Brayden will hopefully be out of the hospital soon."

She smiled. "And then where will that leave us?"

"Wherever you want it to."

"Well, it leaves me right here in Ventura."

"And I'm only around one hundred miles away in Laguna Beach. It doesn't take long to get here."

Audrey knew that it was more than two hours on the road, but then he was used to hopping in a plane, so perhaps, for him, it didn't take long.

"I'd like to keep seeing you, Audrey. I thought we'd have this whole week at the lake and that by the time we left, it would be a natural continuation when we came home. This changes things a little, but it doesn't have to."

She looked into his eyes; they shone as he smiled. "You'd seriously already thought about what might happen after we came home?"

"Very seriously."

The butterflies took to flight again in her stomach, and for a moment, she felt guilty. She shouldn't be sitting here with him, talking like this while Brayden was lying in the hospital.

"Of course, what's happened with Brayden takes priority over everything else."

There he went, reading her mind again!

"But I'd like for us to keep seeing each other as much as you're comfortable with."

"I want you to go back to Summer Lake tonight."

His smile faded, and she had to laugh. "If it were for my sake, I'd keep you here. But you're visiting your family—your grandson. That's important."

He nodded. "You're right. It is."

"And besides. I'd feel guilty if you stayed here. We both have family we need to spend time with."

"We do. I know it's for the best if I leave soon, but only if you tell me when we can see each other again."

She'd love to ask him to stay, but it just wouldn't be right. And she'd love to tell him to come back here this weekend, but she didn't know what state Brayden was going to be in. She'd bring him here with her as soon as he got out of the hospital. So, having Ted come wasn't a great idea. She gave him a sad smile. "I can't tell you, not until I know what's going on with Brayden."

"I know. I shouldn't have asked, but I don't want to leave things open-ended between us."

"Neither do I. How about I call you tonight? It won't be the same as going out or sitting on the balcony at the lodge, but we can talk for a while."

He smiled. "I'd like that. I'd like it a lot."

"Okay, then. We have a deal."

After they'd dropped the rental car off, Audrey walked with him across the airport building. He could see Smoke standing over by the door that led out to the tarmac.

He stopped and put his hands on her shoulders. Looking down into her eyes made his heart race. It wasn't even the fact she that was so beautiful, it was what he saw in her eyes that made him feel this way. She was strong, she was a kind, she was the kind of woman he hadn't believed existed outside of movies. He dropped a kiss on the tip of her nose, and she smiled.

"I'm going to miss you, Ted Rawlins."

He liked the way his name sounded on her lips. "I'm going to miss you, Audrey..." He'd heard the doctor call her Mrs. Patterson. He wondered if that was still her married name.

She smiled. "I never told you, did I? It's Patterson."

"Mrs. Patterson?"

She shook her head rapidly. "Hell, no! Richard's name, the name I used all those years, is Tanner. I gave the name back when I gave the ring back."

He couldn't help smiling. It was petty, but he didn't want to call her by Richard's last name. "Well, I'm going to miss you, Audrey Patterson. But not for long. We'll talk tonight. You can tell me how Brayden's doing. I hope we'll talk every night until I can see you again." He slid his arms around her waist and pulled her into a hug. He wanted to kiss her, but it wouldn't be right here.

She hugged him back and reached up to plant a peck on his lips. "Thanks, Ted. I don't like to think how today would have worked out without you. I'll text you when I get back from the hospital, and you can tell me what time works for you. I hope we will talk every night." She gave him a rueful smile. "But I need you to know that if you change your mind, I'll understand. I'll always treasure these few days and what you did today, especially."

He hugged her closer. "I won't change my mind. We're just getting started."

"I hope so."

She stepped away from him, and he reluctantly let her go. Smoke was waiting, and he could see that Izzy had just come into the building to collect Audrey. It was time. He couldn't resist stealing one last chaste kiss. "See you soon."

Smoke greeted him with a smile. "It looks like everything's okay?"

"Yeah. Her son isn't nearly as bad as we feared."

"That's good news." Smoke watched Audrey walking away. "This wasn't just you being a good Samaritan, huh?"

"No." Ted watched as Audrey reached Izzy, and the two of them turned and waved at him. He waved back with a smile. "This is a whole lot more than that."

Smoke smiled. "That much is obvious. I was hoping you'd tell me what it is."

"I would if I could. I don't know myself yet."

"But you're hoping it's going to be something big?"

"I am."

It was only four-thirty by the time they landed back at Summer Lake. It was hard to believe that despite everything that had happened, he wouldn't even be late to Eddie and April's house.

After he'd thanked Smoke, he got back in the car and headed in that direction. He called Diego on the way.

"How is he?" Diego answered as if they were continuing a conversation that they'd only interrupted a moment ago.

"Nowhere near as bad as we feared."

"That's good news."

"It's a relief."

"Are you still there?"

"No. Smoke brought me back to the lake. Audrey needs to be with Brayden and Ally's with her and ..." He smiled and left the rest of the sentence dangling, wondering if Diego would ask about Izzy.

Diego stayed quiet for a long moment.

Ted outwaited him.

"Was Izzy with her?"

Ted laughed. "Why, yes. She was. Why do you ask?"

"Because she should have someone with her at a time like this—a friend. What about the ex-husband?"

Ted frowned his intention of teasing Diego forgotten. "She spoke to him before we left here. I don't know what he said, but he upset her. He didn't bother to show up at the hospital. Didn't even call his daughter. He didn't even call Audrey again until we were there. Apparently, he's only a few miles down the road."

"You sound angry. Why? Are you jealous of him?"

"No! I have no need to be. Audrey has no feelings for him anymore—well, none other than irritation."

"I'll believe you if you want me to."

"She doesn't!"

"I don't mean about her feelings. I mean about you not being angry. I know you, Ted. You're steady, even-keeled, reasonable. All the things that I am not. But right now, you're angry at this dick she was married to."

Ted had to smile. "Okay. You got me. I can't explain it. I dislike him, that's easy to understand. I have no respect for the way he's treating his kids—but we both know from experience that some people are that way. But you're right. I've had this low-grade anger toward him ever since Saturday night. It's not rational, but ..." he shrugged. "Perhaps you're right, perhaps I am jealous of him."

"Or perhaps you have some sense, some intuition that he will do something to anger you."

"Perhaps. It's likely that he will, given the circumstances."

"I'd say it's more than likely."

Ted turned off the road into Eddie and April's driveway. "I'm at Eddie's now. I said I'd come to see Marcus after school. Is there anything at the office I need to know about?"

"All quiet here. You go enjoy your family time. I'll speak to you in the morning."

"All right. Thanks for today, Diego."

Diego laughed. "There are no thanks ever needed between you and me, mi amigo. We're a team."

"We are. A great team. Talk to you tomorrow."

Chapter Fourteen

"Can I get you anything, sweetheart?"

Brayden smiled. "I'm fine, Mom. Thanks. You really don't need to wait on me, you know. I can get around no problem now."

Audrey knew that he thought she was going over the top taking care of him, and he might have a point. "I'm sorry. I don't mean to fuss over you; I can't help it."

He patted the bed where he was sitting and shifted over so she could come and join him.

She sat down with a smile. "I know you're too old and too independent for me to treat you like a child, but if you can see it from my point of view, it's not often a mom gets to take care of her kids again when they're grown. I'm making the most of it."

He laughed. "I know. I'm not complaining. If it were only about me, I'd be all over it. Let's see, would I rather be at my apartment surrounded by pizza boxes and crumbs or here in the lap of luxury with you waiting on me hand and foot?" He laughed again. "I think you know my answer. But I feel bad. I messed up your vacation." He gave her a sideways glance. "I messed up your time with Ted."

"That doesn't matter. I want to be with you. I need to make sure that you're okay."

"I get that, but even you can't deny that I am okay now. A couple of days in the hospital, a couple of days being fed and waited on by you, and I'm doing better than I have in a long time. And much as we both struggle to realize it most of the time, I'm a grown-up. I don't need to be dependent on you— no matter how much we've both enjoyed playing the roles again for a couple of days. I want to look out for you, too, Mom. I know you like Ted. And I know you've talked to him every night."

Audrey looked away. She hadn't realized that he knew.

He put his hand on top of hers. "And that's not a complaint. He seems like a nice guy. Ally thinks the sun shines out of … him. What I'm trying to say is, I don't want you going putting yourself last again. You did that all our lives growing up. It's supposed to be your time now. I hate thinking that I might be screwing that up for you."

"You're not!"

"You'd still be in Summer Lake with Ted if it weren't for me."

"True. But that doesn't mean you've messed things up for me. You said it yourself. I've still talked to him every night. It's not as though your accident wrenched me away, and I'm never going to see him again."

Brayden smiled. "So, does that mean you're going to go up there this weekend?"

She frowned. "No. I'm not. Why do you think that?"

"Oh. I heard Clay McAdam was playing. I thought you …"

Audrey shook her head. "Izzy?"

He shrugged but couldn't hide his smile. "Don't blame her. It's not her fault."

"It is. I told her that I'd been invited to go. But I also told her that I'm not."

"See, that just makes me feel bad. I'm making you miss out on something you'd enjoy—and on seeing Ted again."

"I'll see Ted again soon enough. I don't need to go back to Summer Lake for that."

Brayden shrugged. "Okay. I don't want you to get mad at me. I just need you to be sure that if you're staying here this weekend, it's because you want to, not because I made you."

She smiled. "I know. It's my choice. So, let's not argue about it. Now, I'm going to make some fruit salad. Do you want some?"

"Well, if you insist."

She laughed. "I do."

She got busy in the kitchen slicing fruit. Brayden was right, of course; she could go back to the lake for the weekend if she wanted to. But she didn't. She meant what she'd told him. It was more important to her to be here with him. Not because she was so worried about him anymore. He was doing fine, the headaches had stopped, and he could get around on his cast without any problems. It was more that she was indulging herself. She hadn't thought she'd ever have either of her kids at home with her again; she wanted to make the most of having him here while she could.

Her phone rang, and she picked it up off the counter, expecting it to be Izzy. She knew that she was another one she'd have to convince that she really didn't want to go back to Summer Lake this weekend.

Instead, Richard's name flashed up on the display. She made a face. He'd called on Wednesday to check on Brayden after he'd been released from the hospital. Why he needed to call her again, she didn't know.

"Hello?"

"Why answer as though you don't know who it is?"

She pursed her lips. It was going to be like that, was it? "Don't start, Richard. What do you want?"

"What do you think? I want to know how Brayden's doing."

She bit back a retort. Why would she think that was the obvious reason when he'd hardly bothered to check? "You can call him. He has his phone."

"Why are you being difficult?"

"I didn't realize I was. He's doing fine; he'd probably appreciate hearing from you. I thought it might be nice if you called him yourself."

"I thought it might be nice if I came over."

"What? Why?"

"To see our son, of course. Tomorrow's Saturday. I could come over. We could grill some burgers and hang out. Like old times."

Audrey frowned. "You really want to do that with him?"

"I do. I know I haven't been there for him and Ally as much as I should."

"Okay. If you want to spend some time with your son, then you're welcome to come here tomorrow. I have plenty of burgers, you can grill if that's what you want."

He sounded so smug when he spoke again. "I knew you wouldn't turn me down."

"Of course not. So, what time do you want to come?"

"Say, noon?"

"That's great. I need to go. But you won't change your mind, will you?"

"I won't. I can stay over if you want, too."

Audrey shuddered. She tried not to use Izzy's word for him too often, but he really was an asshole. "If that's what you'd like."

"I'd like that a lot."

Did he really think that she was going for it? That she'd let him come over and stay here with her?

"I'll see you tomorrow, Audrey. It's been too long."

"Bye." She made a face as she hung up. She finished making the fruit salad and took it through to Brayden in the spare room.

"Thanks, Mom. Are you one hundred percent sure that you don't want to go away for the weekend?"

"Actually. I think I will."

He grinned. "Was that Ted on the phone?"

"No. It was your father. He said he wants to come over and see you."

Brayden made a face. "He's bringing Natalee here?"

"No, but he said he'd be happy to stay over."

Brayden made a face. "He was suggesting that he could stay with you?"

Audrey shrugged.

"Don't worry. You don't need to protect me. I play dumb most of the time when it comes to Dad, but I'm not stupid. He sleeps around on her. I figured he'd try to make a move on you again after last weekend."

Audrey was shocked but didn't want to say anything.

"He probably won't even want to come if he knows you're not going to be here."

"I thought it might be a nice way for you to spend some time with him."

Brayden smiled. "I'm not interested in spending time with him, Mom. And I don't need him here to babysit me if you want to go."

Audrey blew out a sigh. She'd thought she was being clever, getting Richard here by making him think that she wanted to see him and then not being around so that he'd spend some time with Brayden.

"What's up?"

"I think I messed it up."

Brayden popped a blueberry in his mouth. "You didn't. You go to the lake. Let Dad come over. He won't stick around long once he realizes that you're not going to ..." He stopped, and his cheeks turned red.

It made Audrey sad that even Brayden understood his father well enough to know that he was only looking to have sex.

"How about I call him back and tell him that he can't come?"

"It's up to you, Mom. I think you should go to the lake."

Her phone rang again, and she made a face at him. "I'll be back for your dish."

It was Richard again.

"Yes?" she answered.

"I was hoping you might say that. I was calling to ask if you want me to come tonight?"

"No. I don't. And to tell you the truth, I don't plan to be here tomorrow either."

"But you said—"

"I said you could come over and grill burgers and stay the night. I didn't say anything about being here myself."

"But we could—"

"No, Richard. We couldn't."

"You know you want to."

She let out a bitter little laugh. "No. I know I don't want to. In fact, I can't think of anything I want to do less."

"Let me guess, you're still seeing Ted Rawlins?"

"Yes."

He laughed. "Good luck with that. He won't waste much time on someone like you."

"What do you mean, someone like me?"

"You know full well what I mean, Audrey. You're past it. To be fair, you looked pretty good last weekend, all done up like you were, but now I think I about it, you've saved me a disappointment. You might look good in a decent outfit, but I already know what's underneath. Old. Saggy. Like I said. Past it."

"You really are an asshole, Richard." She hung up and braced her hands against the island while she waited to stop shaking. He was only being vindictive, but she couldn't deny that his words stung.

"Hey. Are you all right?"

She turned to see Brayden leaning in the doorway.

She nodded, not trusting herself to speak.

"What did he say?"

She shook her head. She was hardly going to tell him.

"I'm sorry he upset you. And for what it's worth, I'm glad you called him an asshole. He is."

"I wish you hadn't heard that."

"I'm glad I did."

Her phone rang again, and she eyed it warily, not wanting to get into a shouting match with Richard.

"Don't answer if it's him," said Brayden. "He'll only upset you."

She nodded and looked at the screen. It was Ted. She'd been looking forward to speaking to him, but now wasn't the time.

Brayden limped to the counter and looked at the screen. Before she could stop him, he picked it up.

"Hi, Ted … No. Sorry. She's not around. Can I get her to call you back in a little while? … Yeah. Thanks. I'm doing great now. I've told her she should come up there this weekend… Oh. I see … Maybe you should come here, then?"

Audrey stared at him. What was he playing at?

Brayden smiled at her when he spoke again. "You wouldn't be inviting yourself. I just invited you. And since I'm the reason that she's here and not there ... Yeah. Okay. But I'll get her to call you ... I will. Bye."

He hung up and smiled at her.

"What are you playing at?"

"Being helpful. Since he didn't want you to feel pressured to go up there, I suggested that he should come here."

"And what did he say to that?"

"He said he'd love to, but he couldn't just invite himself. You heard my answer to that."

She smiled. She had, and she loved him for it.

"I said I'd get you to call him later. I figured you might need a minute to get over Dad being such an asshole first."

She wanted to tell him not to call his father that but wasn't that much of a hypocrite.

Brayden smiled. "You're welcome, by the way."

She let out a little laugh. "Thank you. I think."

Ted hung up and set his phone down. He'd called a little earlier this evening because he was supposed to be going over to the Boathouse to watch Eddie play. Brayden had surprised him when he picked up and surprised him even more when he'd suggested that he should come to Ventura.

Audrey had already told him that she wouldn't be comfortable coming back to the lake this weekend, and he respected that. It hadn't occurred to him that he might go there to see her instead. He'd love to—it seemed like so much more than three days since he'd seen her. They'd talked every night for hours on the phone, but it wasn't the same as being with her.

He went and stood in front of the windows of his room and looked out at the lake. This place had grown on him since the first time he'd come to visit Eddie. He'd thought it was just a backwater small town, and it was, but it was such a beautiful place, and it was filled with the kind of people he was happy to call friends.

He went back for his phone when it rang and smiled when he saw Audrey's name.

"Hey."

"Hey. I'm sorry I didn't answer before."

"That's okay. It was good to talk to Brayden. He says he's doing much better."

"He is."

Ted had to wonder whether she knew that her son had suggested he should go and visit them. Much as he wanted to see her, he didn't think he should bring it up. "That's good. Do you guys have any plans this weekend?"

She was quiet for a long moment. "No. And I know he invited you here. Sorry about that."

"Sorry? Why?"

"Because you're there with your family."

"I've been here all week."

"And you have plans with your friends tomorrow night."

He smiled. "Those were our plans, not just mine."

"I'm sorry."

"What for?"

"That I messed them up."

"You didn't. We'll have plenty more chances to come and hear Clay sing."

"We will?"

"I hope so." He frowned. "What's wrong, Audrey?"

"Nothing." He heard her sigh.

"You wouldn't lie to me, would you?"

"Not exactly. Saying there's nothing wrong isn't entirely true, it's just that there's nothing I want to tell you about."

He sat down on the bed. "Are you closing me out?"

"No! I don't mean it like that."

"How do you mean it?"

"I ... I talked to Richard earlier."

Ted wasn't surprised. Her ex-husband seemed to be the only thing that ever upset her. "And you don't want to tell me about that?"

"It's ... I'm sorry, Ted. This is what I didn't want to do."

"What is?" His heart was racing. He had no idea what she was talking about, but he'd already learned that whenever Richard's name came up, nothing good ever followed.

"He ... he said some hurtful things. And I know he was only doing it to upset me, but, well, it worked. He's knocked my confidence."

"Your confidence in what?"

"In myself ... and in you."

Ted frowned. No way was he going to let that man come between them. "What did he say?"

"This is going to sound so pathetic. I don't want to need your reassurance, but I do."

"Tell me?" He managed to keep the anger out of his voice. He hoped he sounded encouraging.

"He ... well, he tried to invite himself over here for the weekend."

Ted's hand balled into a fist beside him.

"He said he wanted to come and see Brayden, and then he suggested that he could stay over, too."

"Stay ... with you?"

"That's what he was suggesting."

"I see."

"You know I don't want that."

He did. At least, he believed he did.

"I said that he could. It was stupid."

Ted's heart felt as though it might beat out of his chest. His pulse was thundering in his ears. "You wanted him to stay with you?"

"No! I told you, it was stupid. He was being all smarmy, and I went along with it—just to see how far he'd go, really. He said he'd like to spend the night, and I said he should—thinking that it might be a way to get him to spend some time with Brayden and that it would free me up to come and see you."

Ted felt his shoulders relax.

"He went for it—can you believe that? I don't know where Natalee is, but he would have come and spent the night here. Then he called back and said he could come tonight if I wanted him to. And I had to tell him, I don't want him here at all. That I'd said he could come and stay—with Brayden. That I didn't plan to be here." She blew out a sigh. "When he understood that I'm really not interested, he got mean. Told me that he didn't know what he'd been thinking. That I might look all right dressed up but that he knows what's underneath, and it's not pretty."

The simmering anger Ted had felt toward Richard was about to boil over. "He's an idiot, Audrey. He's just lashing out because he can't have you."

"I know, but he kind of has a point, too. I am old and saggy compared to Natalee. And what he said the other day is true too."

"What?"

"That a man like you wouldn't waste much time with someone like me."

"That's not true, Audrey. It's not true, and you know it."

"But it should be. Why would you want me when you can have any woman you want?"

"You're the woman I want."

She was quiet, and he knew that she wasn't just waiting for him to flatter her with reassuring words.

"You know it's true, Audrey. I know what's underneath your clothes, too—and I love it. I love every inch of you—I plan to show you just how much when I see you again. I told you this the first night we met. You're a beautiful woman. Inside and out—and underneath your clothes. Don't let him get inside your head."

"I'm sorry. I told you I know it's pathetic, but it got to me."

"I understand. I just don't want you to let him shake your confidence, not in yourself or in me—or in us. Okay?"

"Okay. That's why I told you. I don't want to let it eat away at me."

"I'm glad you did. Can I come and see you?"

"When?"

"Tomorrow."

"But—"

"I was going to go out tomorrow night anyway. The only thing I would miss with the family would be breakfast on Sunday morning before I leave, and Marcus hates getting up for that. He won't mind skipping it. I could be in Ventura by six tomorrow evening."

"I'd love for you to come."

"Then, I'll be there."

"I can't wait."

He smiled. "Neither can I." He planned to remind her just how beautiful she was.

Chapter Fifteen

Audrey jumped when the door from the garage opened, and Izzy bounced into the kitchen.

"Jeez! I'm not that scary, am I?"

"You are when I'm not expecting you!"

"Sorry. I was going to call, but I knew that if I did, it would only give you time to think up a more solid excuse."

"Excuse for what?"

Izzy grinned. "To get out of going to Summer Lake. I think we should go."

"Two questions: first, why? And second … we?"

Izzy shrugged. "Why not, and why not?"

Audrey had to smile. "I have a lot to catch you up on, but first, I think you should catch me up on what you're thinking."

"What am I thinking?"

"About Diego?"

"No! Well, maybe a little. But only as eye candy. My real motivation is to make sure that you get to see Ted again. And of course, I wouldn't mind flying in the plane again, and I wouldn't say no to seeing Clay McAdam sing."

Audrey shook her head. "Well, I am going to see Ted again. But he's not sending the plane for me; he's coming here. And I've already told you that Clay is well and truly spoken for. His fiancée, Marianne, is lovely."

Izzy rolled her eyes. "And I have told you that I only want to look. But more importantly, when's Ted coming?"

"Tonight. He's coming here."

"Oh, that's awesome. Good for you."

"I think so."

"What's that look for?"

"What look?"

"I don't know. You look as though you're not really thrilled about it."

"No! I am! It's just …" She hated to admit it to Izzy, but she needed to. "I kind of pulled a needy female on him last night, and he said he'd come here to see me."

Izzy frowned. "What kind of needy female, and why? I don't like the sound of that."

"It's okay. It was just Richard got in my head, telling me that I'm old and saggy and that Ted wouldn't be interested in me for long." She blew out a sigh. "I know he was just being mean, but …"

Izzy's eyes were wide. "You told Ted that?"

"I did. It was eating at me, even though I know it's stupid. I thought it was better to tell him than to let it freak me out and change the way I act toward him."

"And it didn't freak *him* out?"

"No. Like I said. He's coming here to see me."

"Wow! I would never have admitted that. Guys freak out and run when they think you're getting needy."

Audrey couldn't resist. "I guess younger guys do."

Izzy narrowed her eyes. "Touché. I'm not going to argue, because I know you have a point. I guess dating someone our age does have some advantages."

Audrey smiled. "I think so. And I know what you think of as the biggest advantage younger guys have—but there's no way they could be better than Ted."

Izzy's eyes grew wide. "In bed?"

She tried to bite back her smile as she nodded.

"Damn you, Audrey! I want to hear all about it, but I know you're not going to tell me."

"Maybe you should test drive an older guy for yourself."

Izzy pursed her lips. "I would love to tell you that I'd never even consider it."

"Ooh. That's what you usually say."

"I know."

"Are you telling me that Diego got under your skin?"

"I hate to admit it, but yes."

"So, you should—"

Izzy held a hand up. "Nope. That's a terrible idea. Don't even say it. And besides, we're talking about your love life, not mine. So, Ted's coming here tonight and … then what?"

"I don't know. We're going to play it by ear."

"I like the sound of that. My guess is that you two are going to get serious."

Audrey smiled.

"I think you will, too."

They both turned to see Ally standing in the doorway.

"Everyone's just sneaking in here today!" exclaimed Audrey. "How long have you been there?"

Ally smiled. "Long enough to hear that Ted's coming here tonight … and to agree with Aunt Izzy that you guys are going to get serious. And by the way … I approve."

"Well, thanks." Audrey wanted to feel indignant that her daughter had overheard the conversation, but she didn't. She was too thrilled that both she and Izzy were so enthusiastic about her relationship with Ted.

~ ~ ~

Ted spotted her as soon as he came through the doors from the tarmac. He got the same feeling he had when he was a kid on a date. It made him smile. He'd have said he was too old to feel that way, but he liked it.

She smiled and started toward him when she saw him. He closed his arms around her and landed a peck on her lips. "Hey."

"Hi."

He could feel her heart beating in her chest. "Are you nervous?"

She nodded. "I am. It felt so strange standing here waiting for you."

"Strange in a good way?"

"The best." She took hold of his hand and led him out to the parking lot. "I'm so glad you're here."

"I'm glad you wanted me."

When they reached the car, he threw his bag onto the back seat and met her gaze as she watched him. He knew what she must be thinking. "I'm not assuming that I get to stay the night with you. But I brought my bag just in case. Karl's standing by. He'll fly me home after we have dinner, or if you want to see me tomorrow, I can get a room at the Marriott for the night."

She smiled. "You're going to make me say it, aren't you?"

He raised an eyebrow.

"I'd like you to stay … with me, not at the Marriott."

He closed his arms around her. "I didn't want to assume. I didn't know if you'd be comfortable with it. With Brayden being home."

She chuckled. "Brayden's not home. Izzy and Ally were both over this afternoon, and when they found out you were coming, they decided that Brayden should stay at Izzy's tonight."

Ted had to laugh. "I want to be happy that they're giving us some time alone. I'm just a little concerned that they all took off when they knew I was coming."

"Oh, they wanted to see you. In fact, they're hoping that they will tomorrow. I don't know what time you need to leave …" She left the question hanging.

"The only thing I have to do is be back in the office on Monday morning. So, I'll stay until you want rid of me."

She looked up into his eyes, and he wanted to tell her the same thing he'd told Izzy—that he'd be with her for as long as she wanted him. But he held back. Maybe later.

She made him a wonderful dinner, and afterward, they sat out on the patio by the pool with a glass of wine.

"Thanks for coming, Ted."

He laughed. "You're more than welcome. You know I could hardly wait to see you again."

"I do, but you weren't planning on it being this evening. You're only here now because I went all needy on you."

He frowned. "Needy? When? I missed that."

She smiled. "You know what I mean. Last night, when I told you what Richard had said."

That now-familiar anger bubbled up. "Ah. That. I didn't think you were being needy. You were being honest with me. And you know I always want you to be honest. I'm glad you told me about it. It'd be too easy to let him get inside your head, make you doubt."

"It would. I couldn't get past what he said. I wanted to. I knew it was stupid to let him upset me, but ..." She looked away. "He does kind of have a point."

"About what?"

"About me being ... older. Less attractive. I'm not putting myself down. I'm just being realistic."

He got up from his chair and went to squat down in front of her. He took hold of both of her hands and looked up into her eyes. "I can't argue that you're older. But to me, that makes you more attractive, not less. I'll never stop telling you that you're beautiful ..." He traced her cheek with his finger. "because you are. You compared yourself to his wife. You think that she's more attractive because she's young. To a man like Richard she might be. But you need to understand, Audrey, men are attracted to younger women when they're not ready to let go of their youth. They don't want to step into the next chapter of their lives—or they're afraid of reaching the final chapters. I don't feel that way. I'm happy with who I am and where I am in life. I'm not searching for something or trying to reclaim anything. I want to enjoy being who I am, and I want to enjoy having a woman I respect beside me. You're beautiful, inside and out."

A single tear rolled down her cheek, and he reached up and wiped it away. "I didn't mean to upset you."

"You didn't. That's a happy tear."

"Does that mean you want to be the woman by my side?"

She nodded.

"Good. Then tomorrow, can we talk about how we make this work? I want to be by your side as much as possible."

She looked a little disappointed.

"If you're wondering why tomorrow and not now, it's because I have other plans for right now." He trailed his finger down between her breasts, loving the way they rose and fell, and her nipples stood to attention under her shirt.

She raised an eyebrow. "And what exactly are you planning?"

"Well." He got to his feet and offered her his hand. "Since everyone made a big deal of making sure we have the house to ourselves tonight, I think we should make the most of it, don't you?"

Her eyes sparkled as she nodded and led him inside.

~ ~ ~

It was strange to see him in her bedroom. She'd deliberately decorated it to be a completely feminine space. Ted looked rugged, strong, and so very masculine by contrast. It sent shivers down her back.

She stopped when she reached the bed and looked up into his eyes. He held her gaze for a long moment, and she could feel the words he wasn't saying. He thought she was beautiful, and he wanted her.

She looped her arms up around his neck. "I've missed you, Ted."

"I've missed you more."

"I've imagined this moment."

He smiled. "You have? And how did it go?"

"Very, very well."

"Want to guide me through it?"

She gave him a puzzled look.

"Tell me how it went, what you enjoyed. What you want."

A wave of heat surged through her and settled between her legs. She swallowed.

He lowered his head and claimed her mouth in a kiss that left her panting. "Tell me," he breathed. His hands were moving over her, making it hard to focus.

She drew in a breath to steady herself. "You undressed me."

He got rid of her skirt and top so that she stood before him in her underwear. "Like this?"

She nodded as she watched him undress. His muscled thighs reminded of her of the first time she'd seen him in the gym at the lodge.

"What else?" he asked when he straightened up.

She sat down on the bed and held her arms up to him. Was she really going to tell him?

He lay down beside her and claimed her mouth again. His hands moved over her, and by the time he came up for air, their underwear was gone.

He leaned back and let his gaze travel over her. Her hands automatically came up to cover her breasts, but he shook his head. "Please? Let me see you?"

She let her hands fall away and a little moan escaped from her lips when he cupped her breasts. His thumb made it hard for her to concentrate as it circled her nipple. She let her head fall to the side, wanting to enjoy the sensations that were rolling through her, but not wanting him to—

"Come back to me."

She met his gaze, and he increased the pressure, sending shock waves racing through her.

"I want us to enjoy each other, Audrey. I don't want to touch you and make love to you while you hide in your head. I want you to stay here with me." His hand moved down over her stomach, and she gasped as it slid between her legs. "I want you to come for me. I want to share this with you."

She bit down on her bottom lip as his fingers slid inside her. He held her gaze and rubbed his palm up and down over her clit as his fingers moved in and out. She wanted to look away, but she understood what he was asking her. Letting him touch her was one thing; this was another level of intimacy.

He slid his leg between hers and opened her up so that he could go deeper. She grasped a fistful of sheet underneath her, and couldn't help moving her hips in time with him.

A hint of a smile touched his lips. "Does it feel good?"

She nodded breathlessly.

"What else did you imagine me doing here?"

She closed her eyes briefly. Could she tell him?

His smile grew wider. "Tell me."

She could barely form words. His talented fingers were taking her closer and closer to the point of no return. "This is good."

He withdrew his hand, and she shook her head. "No." She didn't want him to stop.

He moved down until his face was between her legs.

She nodded. "Yes. That's what you did."

He smiled. "What?"

"You … tasted me."

She closed her eyes and let out a low moan when his hot wet tongue trailed over her entrance and then dipped inside.

She now had two fistfuls of sheet, and when his mouth closed around her clit, her back arched up off the bed.

He lifted his head, so he could see her face. "Did you come for me?"

She nodded breathlessly and then gasped when his fingers pushed at her again. This was so much better than what she'd imagined! His tongue teased her, and then his fingers sank deep. Her hips rocked in time with him. He was taking her to the edge … and over. "Oh, God! Ted!" She gasped as her orgasm tore through her. She saw stars as his tongue, and his fingers refused to let up. Her whole body quivered through what might just be the best orgasm of her life.

When she finally lay still, he wrapped her up in his arms and claimed her mouth in a kiss that soon had her panting again. She opened her eyes when he rolled onto his back, pulling her with him so that she was on top.

His smile was still kind, but it had a wicked edge to it, too. She slid her hand between them and closed her fingers around him. He was hot and hard. She moved him against her, and he rocked his hips.

She'd thought she was spent, but being up here like this had her ready to go again. He thrust his hips harder, and she gasped as he pushed at her slick entrance.

"Sit up," he breathed.

She shook her head. She wanted to ride him, but she didn't want him to have a full-frontal view of her while she did. Richard's comment about her being saggy still echoed in her head.

"Please?"

She closed her eyes. She couldn't deny Ted anything when he looked at her like that. She sat up, resisting the urge to cover her breasts with her hands. His hands grasped her hips. His eyes held her gaze, and he thrust his hips—not hard, not fast, but a slow, inexorable movement of his cock deeper and deeper inside her. She felt every inch of him, and his eyes never left hers. She felt connected to him in every way possible. His hand came up to touch her breasts which were rising and falling on her ragged breaths.

"Come with me, Audrey."

She nodded, and they began to move together, slowly at first and then with more urgency. He grasped her ass, and she bounced up and down, taking him deeper and deeper until she couldn't take any more. He took her over the edge, and she saw stars as a wave of pleasure crashed through her. He held her gaze the whole time, and she saw the moment that he found his release just before she felt it.

"Audrey!" he gasped, as their bodies melded frantically into one.

She slumped down on his shoulder, and he turned and pressed a kiss into her hair. "You're amazing, Audrey Patterson."

She smiled. "Correction, Ted Rawlins. We are amazing."

"We are." He looked as though he was about to say something else, but instead, he smiled. "We sure are."

Chapter Sixteen

Audrey set a mug of coffee down in front of him, and Ted caught her wrist with a smile. "Thank you."

She stepped closer. "It's the least I can do after all you've done for me."

He pulled her arm so that she sat down in his lap, and he closed his arms around her. "I've done nothing."

She laughed and wriggled in his lap, making him stir for her—but after everything he had done, stirring was all he could manage yet. "You know what I mean."

"I do." He brushed his lips over her neck. "But, you've done as much for me, too."

He loved the way she smiled; she looked different. They'd spent the rest of last evening in bed, and most of the night on and off, exploring each other, getting closer in every sense. This morning she was more relaxed with him, but perhaps, more importantly, she was more relaxed with herself.

"I'm glad you liked it."

A shiver tickled the back of his neck at the memory. He hadn't expected her to do what she'd done this morning. "Like is such a weak little word." He winked at her. "I loved it." His breath caught in his chest. There he went again! He wanted to tell her that he loved her. That was crazy. It was way too soon. Though, looking at her, the way she was smiling at him, the way she felt in his lap, in his arms, it didn't feel crazy. It felt natural.

She held his gaze. "What are you thinking?"

He froze. He could hardly tell her that he was figuring out that he was in love with her and debating with himself whether it was too soon to tell her.

Luckily, she laughed. "I knew it. You're hoping that I'll do that again, aren't you?"

He gave her a rueful smile. It wasn't what he'd been thinking, but he couldn't wait for her to do it again.

She checked her watch. "Now?"

He laughed. "No. I can wait."

"You know the kids and Izzy are going to be here in a while." Her smile faded. "If not now, then I don't know when we'll get the chance again."

He brushed her hair away from her cheek. "Relax. We'll see each other again soon. I don't have to leave tonight. I can go straight to work from here in the morning if you want me to stay—if it's not too awkward with Brayden."

She frowned. "I'd love for you to stay again, but …"

He nodded. He wasn't sure how he felt about sleeping in her bed with her son just down the hallway. Hopefully, the time would come when it wasn't a big deal, but maybe tonight was too soon still. "Whatever you're comfortable with. Before I leave here, we'll set up when we're going to see each other again. If it were up to me, I'd take you back to Laguna Beach with me and keep you there." It was true, but he knew he shouldn't have said it.

She laughed. "It sounds wonderful, but I have Brayden, and I have to go to work."

"I know."

"You were only joking, then?"

He squeezed her hand. "Honestly? I was completely serious, but there are some practical realities to work out between now and the day when I can ask if you'd like that."

Her eyes widened, but she didn't look horrified.

"Too much?" he asked.

She shook her head slowly. "I feel as though I should say that yes, it is or, at least, that it's too soon, but ..." She smiled and dropped a kiss on his lips. "It makes me feel hopeful."

"I'm hopeful that that's where we're heading, Audrey."

She kissed him again, and this time, he tangled his fingers in her hair and pulled her down so he could kiss her more deeply.

~ ~ ~

"He's awesome, Mom."

Audrey smiled at Brayden, who was standing beside her in the kitchen. She'd come in for more buns and salad. "I think so."

Brayden laughed. "Yeah. That much is obvious. You're as besotted with him as he is with you, and that's saying something."

"Besotted?"

"Yup. I can see why Dad's so jealous, too. You two just seem like you fit together. You're like one of those celebrity couples."

Audrey laughed. "I don't know about that."

"I do. I hope this works out for you."

"Thanks. I do, too. Shall we get back out there?"

"Sure."

She let Brayden go ahead of her. He was doing well on his cast. He said he wanted to go back to work tomorrow, but she wasn't sure that was a good idea.

She set the buns down on the table next to the grill, where Ted was flipping the burgers.

"They won't be long now."

She went to him and pecked his cheek. "Thanks. I didn't just bring you here to play barbecue chef for me, you know."

He winked at her. "I know."

She tried to hide her smile. They both knew he'd done so much more for her than that.

"He is a very good barbecue chef, though," said Izzy. "These burgers are delicious. I vote you keep him on."

Ally smiled at Audrey. "I do, too. Make it permanent."

Audrey glanced at Ted, but she wasn't worried that it might be too much for him. Instead, he grinned at her. "See, I come with recommendations from your nearest and dearest and everything."

"I'll add my vote, too," said Brayden.

Ted looked down at Audrey. "I'm at your service if you want me."

She held his gaze for a moment, and when he laughed, she knew he understood what she was thinking—she wanted him all right.

"It's a shame that you guys missed out on seeing Clay McAdam play last night," said Ally when they were all seated at the big table on the patio.

Audrey shrugged.

"There'll be other chances," said Ted. "We can all go up next time he's playing if you like."

"I'd like," said Izzy with a grin.

Ted narrowed his eyes at her. "Am I allowed to ask if you want to go and see Clay or ..."

Izzy laughed. "I like to look! I know Clay's engaged."

"Nicely sidestepped on the or ... Izzy," said Audrey. "But, I'll let you off the hook because I just remembered something. Ally, I should have told you as soon as I got home, but this week has been a little crazy. You need to call Marianne."

"Marianne?"

"Clay's fiancée."

Ally's eyes widened.

"She's thinking about hiring a wedding planner," Audrey explained.

"Oh my God! Mom! And you forgot to tell me? She's marrying Clay McAdam? That could be one of the biggest weddings of the year!"

"No! She only wants something small and intimate."

"It doesn't matter!" Ally was up on her feet. "Once you work with someone like that, you're in! What's she like?"

"She's lovely. Very down-to-earth. I think you'll like her."

"I know I will." Ally laughed. "I already do! Do you have her number? Did you tell her I was going to call? Oh, no! You've been home all week. She might think that I'm not going to call. She might have found someone else in the meantime!"

Audrey's heart sank. She could only hope that Marianne hadn't done that. "I'm so sorry, sweetheart. I'll give you her number now."

"Thanks."

Ted gave Ally a reassuring smile. "I don't know for sure, but I saw Marianne and Clay on Friday night, and he was teasing her that perhaps she didn't want to marry him after all. It didn't sound as though she'd found anyone to help her out."

Ally blew out a big sigh. "I so hope you're right. I'd love to get that job." She made a face at Audrey. "I haven't said anything yet, but I'm so ready to leave Carina."

Audrey nodded. "I'm not surprised. She takes advantage of you."

"I know. I put up with it while I was paying my dues, but ... I can't take it much longer. I need to find my own clients and strike out on my own. Summer Lake would be an awesome place to start, too."

Ted smiled at her. "I can't promise anything, but I might be able to hook you up with another client there, too."

"Who?" asked Ally eagerly.

"My son, Eddie, and his fiancée, April."

"Hmm." Ally didn't look too impressed, and Audrey had to wonder what her problem with that idea might be. It was sweet of Ted to suggest it.

When she realized they were all looking at her, waiting for an explanation, Ally smiled. "I'd love to help them! Eddie's been a friend for years, and April's a sweetheart."

"But?" asked Ted.

Ally made a face. "I offered my help if they needed any—for free, of course, as a friend, but April said she'd love my help. But she couldn't accept it. I'd have to stay up there at least some of the time, and that doesn't come cheap." She shrugged. "I guess they have to watch their budget; I mean, Eddie's in the band, but he doesn't exactly have the same budget as Clay McAdam."

~ ~ ~

Ted smiled politely, but he couldn't help but wonder what Eddie and April's real reasons were. Ally obviously didn't know it, it seemed very few people did, but Eddie could afford to hire the best wedding planner in the country if he wanted. Ted had been absent for way too much of his life, and he knew that money could never make up for that, but he'd made sure that Eddie was taken care of. His trust fund ensured that he'd never have to work a day in his life if he chose not to.

Audrey cast a glance at him, but he couldn't guess what she was thinking. He hated the thought that she might be wondering about Eddie and April's supposedly meager wedding budget when he was as undeniably wealthy as he was.

He winked at her, hoping she'd understand that he'd explain it to her later. Then he smiled at Ally. "If April wants your help, then she should have it. I'd be happy to pay you the going rate. I can call it part of my wedding gift."

Audrey gave him a wary look. "That's kind of you, Ted, but I think you should let April decide if she wants the help first."

He smiled. "Of course. I'm not meddling. I know better than that. I'm just saying that if the cost is the only barrier, then it doesn't need to be."

"Thanks, Ted." Ally blew him a kiss. "You're the best."

Izzy raised her glass to him with a smile. "Even I have to admit that you're kind of awesome. Here's to you, Ted. I know I can speak for all of us, especially Audrey when I say thank you for coming into our lives."

His heart felt like it might overflow as they all raised their glasses to him. Audrey held his gaze for a long moment, and at that moment, he knew that whenever he wanted to tell her he was in love with her, it wouldn't be too soon.

Brayden grinned at him. "Welcome to the family."

Ally laughed. "Don't freak him out, Brayden!"

Ted wanted to tell them that it didn't freak him out at all. It made him happy. But Ally's next words made him even happier.

"We love you, Ted!"

He knew it was only a phrase, but it still made his heart buzz in his chest as he smiled around at them. "Thank you. Thank you all." He looked at each of them in turn and waited until he was looking into Audrey's eyes before he added. "I love you, too."

Her eyes widened, and so did her smile. She didn't say anything, but a hint of pink touched her cheeks, and she raised her glass a little higher and nodded.

"Well, isn't this cozy!"

Ted spun in his chair to see Richard standing in the doorway from the kitchen.

Audrey sprang to her feet. "What are you doing here?"

"I came to see our son. I thought you were eager that I should spend more time with him. Or are you trying to get poor Ted to fill in for me?" He shot a glance at Ted, who got to his feet and went to stand beside Audrey, putting his arm protectively around her waist.

"Just leave, Dad." It was Ally who spoke first. She came and stood between Richard and Audrey. "You were never here when we wanted you to be. So why show up now that we don't?"

Richard glared at her.

To Ted's surprise, Brayden came to stand beside him. "She's right, Dad. You should go."

Richard turned on him. "Even you? It doesn't surprise me that those two," he jerked his head at Audrey and Ally, "would suck up to him just because he's loaded, but I thought you'd have more sense."

"I have more sense than you give me credit for, Dad. We don't like Ted because he's got money—you're the only one who thinks how much money a person has defines who they are. We like him because he's a good person, he's kind, he cares about us, and he makes Mom happy. None of which I can say about you."

Richard's face turned red while Brayden spoke, and when he finished, he stepped toward him. Ted stepped forward without even thinking.

He was a little taller than Richard, and he had no doubt that he could overpower him if necessary, but even with the adrenaline surging through his veins—even with the almost overwhelming desire to punch him—he knew that he needed to de-escalate the situation. "I think you should go."

Richard laughed. "You have your arm around *my* wife, and you're defending *my* kids—and you think I should go? Who the fuck are you to—"

"I am not your wife!" exclaimed Audrey. "Ted's right. You need to leave. Perhaps you should go and find your wife."

"Yeah," agreed Ally. "And I'm not your daughter anymore, either."

Richard swung his head to look at her. "Of course, you are, you little bitch."

Ted couldn't take it anymore. He took hold of Richard's arm and twisted it up behind his back before the guy even reacted.

"What? What the …? I'll have you for assault! Let go of me!"

Ted smiled grimly at him. "There's no assault going on here. Just a little friendly persuasion. You've been asked to leave. I'm helping you to make the right choice." He started walking him back toward the house and glanced at Audrey on the way. She gave him a brief nod.

"You expect anyone to believe that this is friendly persuasion? I'll sue you." Richard spoke in a strangled voice. Ted released a little of the pressure on his arm but kept marching forward toward the front door.

He spoke in a low voice close to Richard's ear. "Try me, and you'll find out what my version of unfriendly looks like."

The others all followed them out into the driveway. Once they were there, Ted let go of Richard and gave him a little shove toward his car.

Richard glared around at them all. Ted glared back at him until he looked away and turned his venom on Audrey. "You haven't heard the last of this."

Audrey blew out a sigh. "Can we just let it go? You moved on years ago. Now, I have as well. There's no need for us to ever run into each other again. Your relationship with the kids is yours to figure out."

"And I don't want one," said Ally.

Ted felt bad for Brayden as he looked at his father and shook his head sadly. "Honestly, Dad, neither do I." He came and stood beside Ted again.

Ted felt the urge to put his arm around Brayden's shoulders. The kid was shaking—he could see it. But he knew that would only aggravate the situation. He'd do whatever he could to support him later when it wouldn't be throwing gas on the dumpster fire that was happening right now.

Richard got into his car and reversed out of the driveway with a screech of tires. Once he was out on the road, he put his window down before he pulled away. Ted tensed, wondering what he was going to say—how much he was about to hurt his kids.

To his surprise, Richard looked straight at him and yelled, "You're welcome to them! All of them." And then he drove away.

They stood there for a few awkward moments. It was Izzy who broke the silence. She gave a shaky laugh and smiled at them. "Well, that was fun. Who wants some ice cream?"

Ted was grateful to her for the diffusing the tension, and he laughed with Audrey and the kids as Izzy herded them back inside.

Chapter Seventeen

Audrey parked close to the entrance of the airport building. She hadn't ever been here before last Tuesday; now, she felt like she was a regular. She looked across at Ted and smiled.

He squeezed her hand. "Let's get out, can we? I know you don't want to come in with me, but I want to give you a hug."

She met him in front of the car, and he closed his arms around her. "It's been quite a weekend, huh?"

"It has. I can't apologize enough or thank you enough for ... Richard."

His arms tightened around her. "You don't need to, either. I want to say I'm glad I was there, but we both know that me being there was what antagonized him."

"It was, but I'm kind of glad it happened. It brought things to a head, and that's needed to happen for a while. I've tried to be civil with him for the kids' sake, but after what happened yesterday, I know there's no point in trying to pretend for them." She smiled.

"What?"

"I'm just remembering before we spoke on Friday night— just before Brayden took your call—I told Richard he was an asshole. Brayden heard me, and I felt bad about that—but he told me he was glad that I'd finally said it."

Ted smiled. "Brayden's a good kid. I'd guess he's tried to keep the peace since Ally's more vocal."

"Yep, that about describes their whole life. I thought twins were supposed to be very similar; those two are opposites, but they complement each other perfectly." She laughed. "Between the two of them you get one well-rounded person."

"They're two admirable people. I like them both very much."

"They like you, too."

He dropped a kiss on the tip of her nose. "I like their mother even more."

She smiled up at him. "Their mother thinks you're something special." She hated to do it, but she checked her watch.

Ted chuckled. "You need to get going. I know."

"I'm sorry. I'm just a little tense. I have to get Brayden to work, and then I need to get into the office. Izzy's opening up again this morning, but I was gone all last week." She rested her head against his shoulder. "I wish you didn't have to go. I wish I didn't have to get to work, but we do." She looked up at him. "I suppose this is the point where the rubber hits the road—where we figure out if we can make this work once real life sets back in."

"We can. There's nothing to figure out, Audrey. We can and we will. The only thing that could stop us is if you don't want this."

"I do."

His eyes widened, and she felt his heart thundering in his chest as she leaned against him. Crap! Had those two words conjured up the same thing in his mind as they had in hers?

She knew that most men weren't interested in getting married—she wasn't either. She didn't want to scare him off.

"I want you, I want us to keep seeing each other," she clarified.

His hand came up and cupped her cheek, and he claimed her mouth in one of those kisses that left her breathless—and not just because it took her by surprise; he hadn't kissed her like that in public before.

When the kiss finally ended, he rested his forehead against hers and looked deep into her eyes. "I do."

It made her heart race. It sounded as though … no. She was getting carried away. She had to be. Men like him weren't looking to get married. She knew that. And besides, there was no need. They were going to keep seeing each other. That was enough.

He stepped away from her and opened the back door to get his bag. "I'd better let you go. I don't want to make you late."

She nodded. He was right, but she didn't want to say goodbye.

He tucked his fingers under her chin and planted a peck on her lips. "Call me tonight?"

She nodded.

"And I'll come back for you tomorrow."

She smiled. "I can't wait."

It was five o'clock before Ted finally leaned back in his chair. He'd had a lot to catch up on after not being here all of last week.

He looked up at the sound of a knock on the door. Diego came and leaned in the doorway.

"Are we done for the day?"

"Yep."

Diego smiled. "You look tired. Is that because you worked too hard today or because you played too hard this weekend?"

"Perhaps a little of both."

"Perhaps you should give up one or the other."

Ted frowned. "What do you mean?"

"Work or play. Perhaps it's time you choose one."

Ted didn't get it. He thought Diego liked Audrey and was happy for them. "Are you saying that you don't think I should keep seeing Audrey?"

Diego laughed loudly. "No! I'm asking if you still feel the need to come in here every day. Wondering why you would want to when it means that you won't be able to see Audrey most of the time."

"Oh." Ted ran his hand through his hair. "I don't know what to say to that."

"Then don't say anything yet. Think about it."

"Are you trying to get me out of here? Did you like it last week when I was gone?"

Diego came in and sat on the edge of his desk. "Ted, Ted, Ted. You know me better than that. Your absence did give me reason to stop and think. But I wasn't glad that you were gone." He grinned. "I missed you. What I was questioning was why I was still here."

Ted leaned farther back in his chair. "What are you saying?"

"We have a good staff, no?"

"The best."

"We're not getting any younger."

Ted smiled through pursed lips. "No, but we're not past it yet either."

"Exactly. So, shouldn't we make the most of life before we are. You were at the lake last week with Eddie and April—and Audrey. It made me wonder why I was here. There is nothing that I do here that I couldn't do from the lake. The same goes for you. Why do we continue to come in here every day like good little soldier ants when our boys are living their lives without us?"

Ted gave him a rueful smile. "I don't have a good answer to that question. I don't know. We come in here every day because it's what we've always done, but you're right; there's nothing we need to be here for. Everything is on the computer, even the meetings. I spent half an hour on a video call with Joel earlier—he's two floors down. I didn't need to be here to do that."

Diego grinned. "So, you agree? It's time for a change?"

"What are you proposing? It sounds to me as though you've already figured out what you want to do."

"I have. I want to get a place at Summer Lake. I want to be there, by Zack and Maria and the—"

Ted grinned. "Is she expecting? Is that what's prompted this?"

Diego shook his head rapidly. "Not yet. But they're talking about it. I don't know what it will mean for them. Zack's job—you know?"

Ted did know. As a pilot, Zack was gone a lot of the time flying.

"I want to be there when they start their family." Diego's eyes shone with tears. "I want to be part of it. I want to be a grandpa."

Ted felt tears prick behind his own eyes. He understood. "Pull yourself together," he said it in as sharp a voice as he could manage, but Diego just laughed.

"I will not. I am emotional at the thought. And that is good."

"It is. It's very good. After all those years when you hardly saw Zack. You need to be there for this next chapter of his life."

"And you should be there in Eddie's life, too."

Ted nodded. He'd like to be. "Are you suggesting that we just … retire?"

"No! No way! We simply rearrange our working lives. We offload some of the responsibilities that don't need to fall to us, and we work from home more. I believe the biggest change we need to make is breaking the habit. We come here because we've done it for so many years. We haven't stopped to question it."

"Until now."

"Exactly."

"Would you move to Summer Lake?"

"I want a home there." Diego smiled. "A home where my grandbabies can come."

Ted had to laugh. "You do realize you'll have at least nine months to wait?"

"Of course, but I want to get settled. I want to test it out. Right now, I can't imagine not spending most of my time here in Laguna Beach. But I have the feeling that once I have a home at the lake, and we don't need to come into the office every day, I'll wonder why I want to spend any time here."

Ted nodded. He'd love to spend more time at Summer Lake, but he also had a reason to want to spend more time here and in Ventura. He planned to pick up Audrey tomorrow night and bring her back to his house for dinner.

Diego was watching him with a little smirk playing on his lips.

"What?"

Diego grinned. "You're wondering how you fit Audrey into this new plan, aren't you?"

There was no point in denying it. "I am."

Diego threw his hands in the air. "You move her to the lake with you. Simple."

Ted laughed. "Nice idea, but not so simple. Her kids are in Ventura; her business is, too."

"I know, but if you're meant to be together, it will all work out."

"I guess. Anyway, it's you who's in a hurry to get a place at the lake. Are you going up there this weekend?"

"I would like to. I was going to ask you. Are you going? Do you need the plane?"

Ted smiled. "Perhaps we should all fly up there together."

Diego's smirk was back, and he raised one eyebrow as he asked. "All of us?"

Ted couldn't resist. "Yes. I want to bring Audrey and Ally and Brayden."

Diego nodded, his smirk fading.

"And Izzy," Ted added with a grin.

Audrey looked out at the ocean and shook her head in disbelief. She was still trying to wrap her head around this place. Ted's home was the most beautiful house she's ever been in. She'd known that he was wealthy—he flew around in a private jet, for goodness sake! He and Diego owned a bank. But that hadn't prepared her for this.

She'd been in some gorgeous homes; some of the agency's clients were very wealthy people, and Richard used to love to schmooze with them. But Ted's place was on another level entirely. It was a huge Spanish style mansion—there really was no other word for it—perched above the ocean. They'd eaten dinner out here on the terrace listening to the waves below. She wanted to pinch herself. After the couple of days that she'd had, she was starting to wonder if she might have slipped into some parallel universe.

Ted came back out with a bottle of wine and poured them each a glass.

She took a big gulp of hers.

He squatted down in front of her and took hold of her hands. "Please tell me what it is—what's bothering you? You weren't quite right on the phone last night, and tonight, you're …subdued. What's wrong?"

She cupped his face between her hands and kissed him. "I'm sorry. It's not you. You are the most wonderful man I've ever known."

His eyes were filled with concern. "Why does that sound like there's a but coming?"

She shook her head rapidly. "There isn't. I'm so happy to be here with you." She looked around. "I have to admit that here is a bit more … more … everything than I expected."

He gave her a rueful smile. "I did wonder. It's no secret that I … I'm … I've been very fortunate financially."

She laughed. "Modest as ever."

He shrugged. "I didn't know how I could let you know what to expect. What was I supposed to say that wouldn't come off as me bragging about my big home on the ocean?"

She touched his cheek. "I'm not holding it against you. I'll admit that I feel a little intimidated, but not enough to make any difference."

"Good." He winked. "Because if you don't like the house, I'll sell it. Get something else that you do approve of."

She laughed. "There's no need to do that. I love the place, okay?"

"Okay. Then I'll keep it."

She loved that he would joke about getting rid of it to make her happy. She stroked his cheek. "Feeling intimidated by your home is only a little part of it. I don't think it would have flustered me so much if I were in a better place. I've had a rough couple of days at work, that's all."

He got up and took her hand, leading her over to a big wicker sofa that looked over the pool and to the ocean beyond. He sat down and pulled her with him to sit in his lap.

"Want to tell me about it?" He rested his hand on the back of her neck, his fingers twisting in her hair.

She wasn't sure she did want to tell him about it. She didn't want to think about it; she'd much rather just focus on the way his arm felt around her waist and the way he was playing with her hair. She sighed. "I should, because it's eating at me, and that's affected me enough for you to notice. I'm sorry."

"I'm not looking for an apology. I want to know if I can help—even if it's only by letting you unload."

She held his gaze for a moment, loving that he was so understanding. Goose bumps raced down her arms at the thought that perhaps, what she was loving was him.

"You make me feel like the luckiest woman on earth."

There went that smile again.

"Okay. When I got to work yesterday morning, I was in for a bit of shock. I've told you I have four staff, apart from Izzy. Well, by the time I got to the office, I only had two."

He frowned. "They left?"

"You could say that. The way I see it, they were poached."

He pursed his lips. "Do I need to guess who the poacher was?"

She shook her head. "Izzy was frantic when I got there. They were both there, emptying their desks. They'd both had a better offer—and that offer was conditional upon them starting yesterday. Apparently, Richard had called all four of them on Sunday evening. He told them that he'd signed a big account over the weekend and needed them straight away. He offered them a fifty percent raise. The two who left haven't been with me that long. The two who stayed worked for us when Richard and I were together—they don't want to work with him again."

Ted sighed. "I'm sorry. This is because of me."

"No! It's no one's fault but Richard's. He just a vindictive …" She shook her head.

"Asshole," Ted finished for her.

She had to laugh. "Yes. That."

"I'm sorry he got back at you like that. Will it be hard to replace them? Will you be able to make new hires and move on?"

She made a face. "I hope so, but I'm going to struggle to cover some accounts in the meantime. But honestly, that's not the worst of it. When Brayden got to work yesterday morning, they sent him home."

Ted frowned. "They don't want him there while he's still wearing his cast? They think it's a liability issue?"

"No. They received a complaint about him and let him go."

"What kind of complaint?"

"They wouldn't tell him. All they told him was the name of the client who'd complained."

Ted raised an eyebrow.

"None other than one of Richard's biggest clients."

Ted shook his head in disbelief. "You think Richard had them complain so that Brayden would lose his job?"

She nodded sadly. "He always had a vindictive streak, but I never thought he'd turn it on the kids. I guess I was wrong. Brayden's always made the peace. I think Richard was most hurt by his reaction on Sunday. So, he got back at him."

"And Ally?"

"Yes. Her, too. Apparently, some woman called Ally's boss Carina and told her that Ally was starting freelancing and attempting to poach her clients."

Ted's jaw was set. She'd never seen him look so angry. "He'd do that to his own kids?"

"Yep. I've spent the last two days fuming. I want to tell him exactly what I think of him, but I had the kids over for dinner last night, and they think, and I know they're right, that we should just let it go. We can't change what he's done; all we can do is recover from it and move on."

"But he can't just ruin your livelihoods like that."

"He can, and he has. But we can get over it and regroup. I'll muddle through till I can make new hires. Brayden doesn't mind taking some time until he's fully recovered anyway, and Ally was getting ready to go out on her own." She shrugged. "It never rains but it pours."

He smiled. "I know the saying goes that into every life a little rain must fall, but this seems more like a deluge."

"We'll be fine. I don't have it in me to get riled up and fight him. The way I see it, the kids will never again have any illusions about their father, which is sad, but it'll save them from any future hurt. And me ..."

"What about you?"

"I suppose if I want to find the silver lining ..." She smiled and dropped a kiss on his lips. "Then I can take this as life showing me very clearly indeed just how lucky I am that I met you, and I'm not married to him anymore."

"I admire you, Audrey. I don't think I could be so forgiving."

She smiled. "Oh, don't get me wrong. I'll never forgive him. I'm being pragmatic. I can retaliate, or I can stew in anger—neither of those will do me or the kids any good. So, we'll just move on."

"I wish I could do something to help."

She touched his cheek. "You are. You're here—or at least, I'm here with you. Knowing I was going to see you tonight helped keep me sane through it all."

He caught her hand and kissed it. "Do you want to go back to Summer Lake this weekend? Ally could meet with Marianne, and I'll talk with April and Eddie to see what they're thinking. And Brayden could come, I know there are a couple of guys up there who work in cybersecurity—Dan Benson might be able to give him some pointers or even hook him up with something. We could rent one of the houses at the resort."

Audrey felt as if her heart might overflow. "You're such a good man, Ted. What did I do to deserve you?"

He held her gaze for a long moment.

He looked so serious that her heart began to beat faster. "What? What's wrong?"

He cupped her face between his hands and brushed his lips over hers. "Nothing's wrong. You asked what you'd done, and I think it's time that I told you—you made me fall in love with you."

Her breath caught in her chest, and her eyes filled with tears. "Too soon?"

She shook her head. "No. Perhaps on someone else's timeline, it would be, but I've fallen in love with you, too, Ted."

The way he kissed her left no doubt that his words were true.

Chapter Eighteen

"Tell me to butt out if you like, but is what's happening between you and Audrey what I think is happening between you and Audrey?"

Ted smiled. "That depends. What do you think is happening?"

Eddie shot a glance at him. "I'm wondering if I'm going to finally get a stepmom."

Ted laughed out loud at that. "A stepmom? Don't you think you're a bit old for one of those?"

"Probably, but it was the most roundabout way I could think of to ask if this is the kind of serious that leads to a wedding?"

Ted swallowed. "What would you think if it were?"

"I'll tell you what most people would think—what they'd say. They'd say you've only known her for a couple of weeks. That's no time at all to get to know someone."

It was true.

Eddie glanced over at him again. They were on their way to collect Marcus from Ethan's house. "Aww! Don't look like that, Dad. I'm not saying that I disapprove. I'm not even saying that it is too soon—just that that's what folks will say. From the little I've seen of her, I think she's great. I like Ally and Brayden—and usually, the kids are a reflection of their parents."

"Or at least one of their parents."

"Are you talking about Mom?"

"No! I'm talking about their father, Audrey's ex-husband. He's an asshole."

Eddie frowned. "Yeah. I know Ally's never had any time for him. What's the story there?"

"Too long and too infuriating for right now. But he might have done me a favor."

"How so?"

"He's the reason that neither of them has a job anymore."

"What? Ally said they had some crazy shit to tell me. I thought maybe you guys had decided to get married or something."

Ted shook his head vigorously. "No! Even I know it's too soon for that. And I wouldn't ask her without talking to you about it first."

Eddie grinned at him. "You wouldn't?"

"No. I need to know that you'd be on board with it."

"Well, I can tell you that I would. I think you should set up a prenup or something, but I'd say that with anyone you met. Not just someone you've only known for a couple of weeks."

"I told you. I'm not planning to ask her yet."

"Good. So, how's her ex done you a favor?"

"Well, since they're both looking for work, I thought maybe I could help them find it here."

"Here? Why?"

"Well, Ally has some possibilities here, some weddings she could help plan—including yours if you and April want to use her—my gift, if you want it. And I thought I could put Brayden in touch with Dan Benson. And—"

"You're rambling, Dad. That's not like you. Why would they want to come here? Why would you want them to?"

Ted blew out a sigh. "Because I want to come here, and that means I want Audrey to want to spend time here ... and if her children were here—"

"What do you mean, you want to come here?"

"I mean, I want to be closer to you, son. I loved being around you guys last week. I want more of that. And Diego and I talked about it, and there's no reason we need to be in the office every day. I want to be part of your life." There, he'd said it.

Eddie pulled the truck over to the side of the road and turned in his seat to look at him. "You do?"

"If you want me. I won't get in the way."

Eddie's eyes shone with tears. "You could never do that." To Ted's surprise, he leaned across the console and wrapped him in a hug. "I want you here. We all want you here. Marcus will be thrilled. April will be, too. We were only talking last night about how much we missed having you around this week. It was so nice having you here last week. It felt ..." Eddie's arms closed tighter around him. "It felt like life was finally right when you were here."

He sat back in his seat and gave Ted a sheepish grin. "So, there's the honest answer. Please, Dad, come and be a bigger part of our lives. And on a more manly note ... absolutely, I think it's a great idea."

Ted had to swallow before he could speak. "Thanks, Eddie."

Eddie pulled the truck back onto the road. "If you tell April I cried, I'll tell her that you did, too."

Ted laughed. "Cried? I didn't see anyone cry. I may have gotten something in my eye. I think you did, too, but nobody cried."

Eddie laughed with him. "This is going to be awesome."

"It is, but don't think that I didn't notice the way you ignored my question about if you want Ally to be your wedding planner."

"Nah. I didn't ignore the question. I was more curious about the reasoning behind it, that's all. You need to talk to April about it. She's holding out on me."

"What do you mean?"

"Apparently, she's had this thing about a big dream wedding since she was a little girl. Obviously, she didn't get that when she married Guy. I want her to have everything she wants when we get married, but she's holding back. I don't know if she thinks it'd cost too much or what she thinks, but I just want us to get on with it, Dad. I want her to be my wife."

Ted nodded. "Would you mind if I talk to her about it?"

"Hell, no! I'd love it."

Ted smiled. "Then, I will. And you don't mind if I help her get whatever it is she wants?"

"No! I want her to have it all! And if you can persuade her to let Ally plan it, that'd be great, too. April has enough on her plate as it is with the bakery and the women's center and her studies."

"She does a lot, doesn't she?"

"I want to say too much, but it makes her happy."

"And her parents won't mind … they won't think I'm overstepping on the wedding?"

"No. They're not close. They'll come. I think. But they won't want to be involved, and there's no way they'd pay for anything."

Ted nodded sadly.

"Don't look like that; she has you. She's always bragging on you." Eddie laughed. "At this rate, you're going to end up with two sons and two daughters."

"What?"

"April will be your daughter-in-law when we finally get married, and then Ally and Brayden …" He shrugged. "If you go down that route."

Ted nodded. "I'll be happy to become a part of their lives, but you're my son, Eddie. You're …" His voice wavered, and he had to stop.

Eddie glanced over at him. "Okay, let's talk football or something before we both start bawling, huh? I know it, and you know it. There's no need to say it."

Ted chuckled. "You're right. Who do you think will go first in the draft?"

~ ~ ~

Audrey gave Izzy a stern look. "Are you going to tell me what's going on between you and Diego?"

"I've told you a dozen times—nothing!"

"It didn't look like nothing this morning. Did you two ... did he spend the night with you?"

"No! I want to be offended that you could suggest such a thing, but ..." She laughed. "But no. He didn't. I went down to get some breakfast, and we ran into each other, that's all. We had something to eat while you and Ted were out for your walk on the beach."

Audrey wasn't convinced. "And what are your plans later?"

Izzy smirked. "I've already told you that, too. I'm going to go to the Boathouse and watch the band."

"Okay. If you insist that there's nothing going on between you, I'll believe you. But we both know that there could be if you wanted it."

"Are you encouraging me?"

Audrey smiled. "Why not, he's a nice guy. And he's Ted's best friend. Call me childish—and it might be—but I think it would be really nice if we could all go out together ... as two couples."

Izzy nodded slowly. "It would. I'll give you that. But you know he's not my type."

Audrey had to laugh. "Diego's every woman's type. You can just tell. He's one of those guys. He's good-looking, and he's charming."

Izzy held up a hand to stop her. "Enough already. I know it! But it's not a good idea. You're right, he's Ted's best friend, and I'm yours. The way I see it, Diego and I are going to run into each other all the time from now on because of you two. I think we should keep our distance."

Audrey frowned. "How's that going to work? We're all going to want to go out together."

"I mean physically!"

"Oh. Right. Okay. I'll drop it, shall I?"

"Yeah. That'd be great."

"Can I ask you one last thing?"

"What?"

"Don't you find him attractive?"

"Phew!" Izzy laughed and fanned herself with her menu. "The man is hot! I'm not denying that."

Audrey laughed. "Okay. Now, at least I know you're being honest with me."

"Would I lie?" Izzy made a face. "On second thought, don't answer that. Instead, you can tell me what the plan is for the rest of the weekend."

"Well, as you know, Ally's over with Marianne, and Brayden's meeting up with Dan Benson this afternoon. Ted called a little while ago and said that April wants to see Ally whenever she's free." She smiled. "I know that we're all coming back here tonight, but other than that, I don't think there is much of a plan. What do you want to do?"

"I'm happy hanging out here." Izzy looked around. They were sitting out on the deck of the Boathouse. "Though we might want to give up our table now that we've eaten. It looks like they're still busy."

Audrey got to her feet. "You're right. We should go."

They walked through the restaurant on their way back out to the square.

"Hey, ladies!"

Audrey smiled at the girl behind the bar. The one they'd met on their first night here. "Kenzie! Hi."

Kenzie grinned. "It's good to see you again. Are you going to be regulars around here?"

Audrey smiled. "I don't know about regulars."

"I think she will be," said Izzy. "I don't know about me, though."

"Why's that?" asked Kenzie.

"She's started seeing a guy who has family here."

"Which guy?" asked Kenzie. "I know everyone around here."

Audrey smiled, not sure that she wanted to say.

Of course, she didn't get a choice in the matter. "Ted Rawlins."

Kenzie grinned! "You and Ted? That's awesome. So, are you Ally and Brayden's mom?"

Audrey nodded. "That's me."

"Cool! So, you're all moving up here? The whole family?"

Audrey wondered what had given her that idea.

Kenzie didn't even wait for an answer. "I told Ally that she needs to talk to Angel over at the lodge. I'll bet she could give her more work than she could handle. The lodge is a great venue for weddings ... they've done a lot of them. I bet they'd love to have a wedding planner they could refer people to. She'll be fine. And I'll bet Dan will set Brayden up with something. And what about you?"

"What makes you think that I'm going to move here?"

Kenzie's smile faded. "Sorry. I'm getting carried away. It's just ... I love Ted. We all do. Oh, I should explain, his son, Eddie, is my husband Chase's best friend. Eddie and April and Chase and me, we all kind of think of ourselves as family because ... well, it doesn't matter. But then Eddie got his dad back. And Ted's the best. I guess I'm just getting carried away. I thought with Ally and Brayden coming up here that maybe you and Ted were going to move here too."

Audrey stared at her for a long moment. Her heart was racing. She certainly didn't hate the idea—but it was Kenzie's idea, not Ted's. She made herself smile. "We haven't been seeing each other very long."

Kenzie laughed. "That doesn't necessarily make any difference. Chase and I spent one night together, and then I left here and never planned to come back. He flew to Nashville when he heard I was in some trouble, and he brought me back here." She shrugged. "Sorry. I get carried away. I want everyone to have a love story like ours."

Audrey couldn't help smiling. She wouldn't mind having a love story like that.

"So, you're married to the other guy in the band?" asked Izzy.

"That's right."

Audrey laughed and looked at Izzy. "You owe me twenty bucks."

Kenzie gave them a puzzled look.

"The night of Ally and Brayden's party. You got up on stage and kissed him before they started to play," Audrey explained. "Izzy thought you were his girlfriend; I bet that you two were married."

Kenzie smiled. "I do that every time before they play." She laughed. "A girl has to mark her territory, you know?"

"I do." Audrey looked at Izzy. "I told you."

Izzy blew out a sigh. "Okay. You were right. I guess I've just never known married folks who liked each other that much before."

"Neither have I," said Audrey, "but the difference between us is that I never stopped believing that marriage could be that way even though it wasn't for me."

Kenzie grinned at her. "If we're taking bets, I'm going to bet that you and Ted end up married. You're perfect for him; I can just tell."

Audrey gave her a puzzled look, wondering how she could tell.

Izzy laughed. "Sorry, Kenzie, but I'm not taking you up on that one. My money's with you, not against you."

Audrey looked at her.

"In fact," Izzy added, "I'd put money on it happening before the year is out."

Audrey shook her head. It was more in wonder than in denial, though.

Kenzie grinned at her. "I guess we'll all just have to watch this space, huh? Sorry, ladies, but I need to get back to it. I hope I'll see you both soon."

"You, too, Kenzie."

They walked across the square in the sunshine, and Izzy slipped her arm through Audrey's. "You don't seem as shocked as I thought you'd be about Kenzie saying that you guys might get married."

Audrey sucked in a deep breath. "Unlike some people, I won't deny the way I feel. He's wonderful, Iz. I know you think I'd be crazy to even think about it—and to be fair, we don't even know if Ted would consider it. But … I know it's way too early to even think about it, but I do like the idea."

Izzy squeezed her arm. "Just because I'm a failure in the marriage department, I don't have anything against it. In the right circumstances, for the right people, I think marriage is wonderful. I think you and Ted are the right people."

Audrey squeezed her back. "Thanks. I thought you'd disapprove."

"Nah. It's not for me, but we're different. You heard me tell Kenzie that I wouldn't be surprised if you guys get married. Ted's great. In fact, I'd say that he's already in love with you."

Audrey tried to hide her smile.

"Oh, my God! He is? He is, isn't he? And you are, too! And you've already told each other?"

Audrey nodded happily. "We have."

"Damn, girl!" She blew out a sigh. "I'm thrilled for you, but I'm going to lose you, aren't I?"

"No! You'll never lose me. We've been best friends forever, that's not going to change."

"I don't mean like that. I mean, Kenzie's right. You're going to move up here."

Audrey shook her head. "No. That's not even on the table."

"Yet. It'll happen, though." Izzy smiled brightly. "And it'll be wonderful! It really will. This is a great place. And maybe we can still work together. I mean, I can work remotely if you still want me."

Audrey stopped when they reached the rental car. "Will you stop? You're getting way ahead of yourself."

"Maybe. Maybe not. But you know ... I think I just hit on something whether you move here or not."

"And what's that?"

"Well, I just said I can work remotely. The others can, too—the ones we have left and anyone new you take on. Maybe it's time to give up the office? The lease is coming up for renewal."

Audrey stared at her. "Can we slow down a minute?"

"Sure. Sorry. But keep it in mind, okay?"

Audrey nodded and opened the car door and got in. She and Ted hadn't talked about living together, let alone moving here together. This was all too premature. But as she started the car, she knew that she wouldn't be able to get it out of her mind—and she was going to give Izzy's suggestion some serious consideration—whether she was moving anywhere or not.

Chapter Nineteen

Ted sat at the head of one of the long tables in the bar. Audrey sat beside him. As he looked around at all the people who sat with them, he marveled at how much his life had changed in such a short time. Not so long ago, he hadn't known half of them. Now, he considered them all his friends and many of them family.

Brayden smiled at him. "Thanks for bringing us up here this weekend. I was pretty bummed about losing my job, but after talking to Dan ..." He let out a low whistle. "This has turned out better than I could have imagined."

Ted reached across and grasped the kid's shoulder. "That's great. I'm happy it worked out for you. What's it going to look like?"

"Well, I'm going to have to find myself a place here. There aren't many apartments, but from what Dan said, I should be able to rent a little house for less than my place in Ventura."

Ted glanced at Audrey. She was smiling, but he could see a touch of sadness in her eyes. For the first time, it occurred to him that he'd helped her children find jobs here but hadn't actually talked to her about spending more time here herself.

He'd hate for her to think that he was playing a part in her being able to see her kids less.

"When do you start?" she asked Brayden.

"Whenever I can get moved up here. Dan's awesome. He works from home most of the time, but with this new project he's setting up, he's opening an office, and there's going to be a few of us working there."

"Well, I'll help with getting you packed up if you like."

Ally grinned at her. "You don't need to do that, Mom. We can help each other out. I have to pack up my place too, and we decided that we might as well share a U-Haul and drive up here together." She looked at Brayden. "Or at least, I'll drive, since hop-along still has his cast on."

"I see. And when do you plan to do that?"

"As soon as we get back. It's not like either of us has a job to go to, thanks to Dad."

Audrey nodded.

Ted put his arm around her shoulders. "Don't worry, I'll get you up here as often as you want to come."

She smiled at him, but he could see that she was feeling down. Why hadn't he thought to let her know his intentions first?

Eddie and April were sitting a little farther down the table, and Eddie grinned at him. "I'm going to have to get up on stage soon. Chase has done all the setup tonight so that I could hang with you guys for a while, but I just want you guys to know how happy I am that you're moving up here. It's going to be awesome having you all around." He punched Brayden's shoulder. "But I have to warn you, Marcus and his buddy Ethan are probably going to bug the life out of you."

Brayden gave him a puzzled look.

"They're both into computers."

"Ah!" Brayden smiled. "That's great. I'll be happy to have them over and let them work with me on my stuff."

Ally groaned. "He's just going to create the same mess here as he has in Ventura, you know this, right, Mom?"

Audrey chuckled. "And there's nothing wrong with that. We should all be comfortable in our own space."

"Yeah, but Brayden doesn't have any space, he just has server racks everywhere and parts of dead computers and circuit boards all over the place."

Eddie laughed. "Then we'll know where to find Marcus and Ethan when we want them."

"And what about you, Ally?" asked April.

"Well, I've got you guys and Marianne and Clay as my first couples. I'm so excited."

"Me, too!" Ted loved seeing April look so happy. "Did you talk to Angel about working with the lodge as well?"

"I did. I love her. She said she'd be here tonight. She reckons they'd be able to put plenty of work my way and she's setting up a meeting with the guy who owns the place on Monday to talk about it all—she's happy to refer me to all their bookings, but she thinks this Ben guy might want to set up some kind of contract, too, which would be great. I hope he's all right."

Eddie laughed. "Ben's the nicest guy you'll ever meet. You have no worries there."

As Ted watched them all chat, he thought about what Eddie had said—that soon he'd have two sons and two daughters. Eddie was his son—his one and only child—but he did love the idea of becoming a father figure in Brayden and Ally's lives, too. And he'd managed to pull April aside this afternoon, too. Once he'd persuaded her to tell him about her dream wedding, he'd managed to convince her that it would make him happy if she'd let him arrange it for her. She was such a sweet soul, and she'd had such a hard life before she met Eddie. Ted already thought of her as family, and soon, she would be his daughter-in-law.

He turned to look at Audrey. She was watching the conversation the same way he was. Though, whereas he was enjoying it and envisioning their future as a family, she was no doubt feeling sad about her family moving away from her. He couldn't believe he'd been such an idiot.

She turned and met his gaze with a smile.

"Would you like to get some fresh air?" he asked.

"I would. Eddie hasn't gone up yet, and I'd like the fresh air after dinner."

Ted started to get to his feet, but a hand came down on his shoulder and pushed him back into his seat.

"Where do you think you're going, mi amigo? You can't leave when I arrive."

He turned and smiled through pursed lips at Diego. "I wasn't leaving."

"I know!" Diego took Audrey's hand and kissed the back of it. "Lovely, Audrey. It's my pleasure." He looked back at Ted. "You were about to ask me what I've been up to today."

"I was?"

"You were." Diego pulled a chair over from the next table and placed it behind them so he could put one arm around Ted's shoulders and the other around Audrey's.

She laughed and gave Ted a puzzled look.

"Don't worry about it. This is just how he is. He gets excited, and he likes to share."

Diego nodded happily. "I am, and I do. I am excited because today I found my new home!"

Ted's heart jumped into his throat. He hadn't expected that.

"I talked to Zack, and he put me in touch with Austin. You should talk to him, Ted. He's good. He was going to show me three places, but I fell in love with the first one. I want it. I'm going to buy it."

Ted raised an eyebrow at him. "Just like that? You want the first one you saw? You don't want to see any more or take your time to figure out if it's the right one for you?"

Diego laughed out loud. "Of all people, I thought you would understand."

Ted shook his head. He didn't even understand what his friend meant.

Diego turned to Audrey and then looked back at Ted. "You want me to believe that you haven't fallen in love at first sight yourself? That you can't relate to my excitement and my happiness?"

Now, Ted understood what he meant. He smiled. "I wouldn't expect either of you to believe that. I can totally relate to how you feel."

Audrey frowned. "I'm very happy for you, but does that mean you're moving here, too?"

Diego grinned. "We all are!" He looked around. "Where's Miss Isobel?"

Ted looked at Audrey; he really needed to tell her what was going on—the plans he had in mind that he hadn't yet shared with her, but that he hoped she'd like.

Izzy was just coming back from the bar, and Diego got up and greeted her with a bow. She made a face and walked past him to come and sit by Audrey.

Ted had to laugh at the look on Diego's face when he straightened up and realized that Izzy wasn't there.

"What's going on, kiddies?" Izzy asked.

Audrey gave her a rueful smile. "It's all go around here. Ally and Brayden are making plans to pack up and move; Diego has apparently just fallen in love with a house and plans to move here, too.

She looked so deflated. Ted felt terrible.

Izzy gave him a puzzled look. "Diego's moving here?"

"Not exactly moving but getting himself a place to be closer to his family."

"You should do that, too," Izzy told Audrey.

"I'd love to but—"

Ted couldn't wait any longer. "I might have a solution to whatever *but* you're about to come up with."

They both turned to look at him. Ted wished that Izzy wasn't looking at him so expectantly. Diego appeared behind them.

"May I have a word with you, Miss Isobel?"

A look of irritation crossed her face, but she got to her feet. "Just one word?"

Diego smiled. "Well, maybe a few."

Ted took hold of Audrey's hand. "Do you want to take that walk now?"

"Yes."

~ ~ ~

They went out over the deck of the restaurant and down the stairs that led to the beach. Audrey couldn't help feeling a little sad. She loved having the kids living so close by in Ventura. She was pleased that they'd both managed to find new jobs so quickly, and Summer Lake was a wonderful place, but still. Life wouldn't be the same. They wouldn't be just around the corner anymore. They wouldn't just come in through the door from the garage and surprise her.

Ted took hold of her hand when they reached the bottom of the stairs. "Are you okay?"

"I'm fine. Sorry. I'm pleased for the kids, but I'll be honest, I'm feeling a little sorry for myself at the thought of them leaving."

He stopped walking and put his hands on her shoulders. "I'm sorry, Audrey. I didn't mean for it to look like this."

"What do you mean? It's not your fault."

He raised his eyebrows. "It is! It's all my fault, but I'm hoping you won't think it's as bad as it seems once I explain."

She looked into his eyes. They were such kind eyes; he was such a wonderful man. It was sweet of him to care so much that she was sad about her kids moving away, but it was hardly his fault.

"I'm the one who helped them both find jobs here."

"Yes, and that's so kind of you. I really appreciate it, and I know they do."

"I'm not looking for thanks. I could have helped them find work anywhere."

She frowned.

"I had an ulterior motive."

Her heart began to beat harder and faster. Ulterior motives were something she associated with Richard—not with Ted. "What do you mean?"

"I'm sorry. I should have told you straight away, but I wanted to give us a little bit more time."

"For what, Ted? I don't understand." She was starting to feel uneasy now.

"Diego told us that he found himself a house here. I want to do the same. I want to get a place here and be closer to Eddie."

She nodded. "That's understandable. But what's it got to do with me?"

"Everything, Audrey. I want to spend more time with him and the family, but I want to spend more time with you, too. When Brayden and Ally both needed work all of a sudden, and I knew of people who might be able to help them out here, it seemed perfect. Once they're here, you'll want to be here more, too. And we can be together more."

He looked so unsure of himself.

"Diego and I talked about not needing to go into the office so much anymore, and about wanting to spend more time with family. I ... I suppose my only reason for not telling you about it straight away is that ... well, I want to be able to think about you and Brayden and Ally as my family, too. But I know it's too soon."

"What are you saying, Ted?"

"That I don't want you to feel sad that they're moving here, because I want you to move here, too ...."

"What would I do here?" Even as she asked, she remembered her conversation with Izzy earlier. She could work from home here just as easily as she could work from home in Ventura.

"I know. It's selfish of me. And I know it's too soon to ask you to live with me."

Her breath caught in her chest. "To what?"

He dropped a kiss on her lips. "I know it's too soon, but whenever you're ready, I would like you to move in with me. If you want to. And then ... down the road ...."

Her heart was pounding in her chest.

"Or did I screw everything up? Is it too crazy?"

"It's not too crazy." She sucked in a deep breath and then slowly let it out. "And, honestly? It's not too soon, either. Maybe it is on somebody else's timeline. But we're on our own timeline. We can do what's right for us. And you're right for me, Ted."

He cupped her face between his hands and brushed his lips over hers. "You're right for me, too." He winked. "Does that mean I can do you?"

She laughed. "Any time you like."

He closed his arms around her, and she rested her head against his shoulder.

"We'll figure it out, Audrey. If it's up to me, I want to wake up beside you every day for the rest of my life. It doesn't matter if that's at your house in Ventura, my house in Laguna Beach, or the house we find ourselves here."

She looked up at him. "I want to agree with you that it doesn't matter, but if we're honest, we both want to be here, near our kids—our family."

He smiled. "We do. And you're happy for us to buy a place here?"

"I'll have to sell mine in Ventura first."

He shook his head. "You don't have to. I know what you're thinking, but it's not an issue, and I don't want you to feel like you have to give everything up to be with me."

"We'll figure it out."

He dropped a kiss on her lips. "We will. I feel as though together, we can make anything possible."

"That's because we can." Audrey couldn't quite believe that this was happening. But she couldn't deny that it felt right.

Ted lowered his lips to hers, and just like he did every time he kissed her, he made her feel as though everything was going to be all right. He made her feel safe even at the same time that he made her feel sexy—and oh, so very loved.

~ ~ ~

Ted was nervous as he waited in the lobby at the lodge on Sunday morning. They'd decided that it was better to stay here rather than at one of the houses in the resort. This way, everyone had their own space and could come and go as they pleased.

He and Audrey had had breakfast with Diego and Izzy—he still couldn't figure out what was going on there. And afterward, Audrey and Izzy had spent some time together. He loved that she had such a close friend. Whenever he'd dated in the past, women hadn't been so understanding about how close he and Diego were. He knew that wasn't an issue for Audrey.

"Hey, Mr. Rawlins."

"Good morning, Roxy. For someone who's not supposed to work weekends anymore, you're here on Sundays a lot."

She shrugged. "I don't mind helping out. And Logan's working, too. We get time off in the week to make up for it."

"Logan runs construction at the development, doesn't he?"

She nodded proudly. "He does."

"Do they build any custom homes?"

She smiled. "They do. Please tell me, you're thinking about moving here?"

He winked and nodded but didn't answer.

She clapped her hands together. "That's wonderful! Oh, I'll give you his card, or he can call you, whatever you prefer."

"Thanks. Roxy, I'll take his card. You can tell him to expect my call soon. I want to get moving on this."

"That's wonderful. Oh, here she is."

Ted turned and his heart clenched in his chest when he saw Audrey coming out of the elevators. He wasn't sure that it was wise to do what he wanted to this morning. But after the mess he'd made of things by leaving it too long to tell her what he was thinking about moving here, he'd decided that he shouldn't delay in telling her what else he wanted. She didn't have to say yes, yet. He just needed her to know how he felt and that he hoped that with time she'd feel that way, too.

She greeted them with a smile. "Hi."

"Morning." Roxy's phone rang, and she scowled at it. "You guys have a wonderful day," she told them before she picked it up.

Ted was glad to be able to take Audrey's hand and go without needing to stay for more chitchat.

"Where are we going?" she asked.

"I thought we could take a walk around the plaza like we did on our first date."

She smiled. "Aww. Aren't you sweet? You're the best boyfriend a girl could hope for."

"I do my best. I'm trying to make you see that I'm a good guy."

She laughed. "I already know that. Everyone who meets you knows that."

They walked down the steps and out across the square.

"Are we going somewhere in particular? You're walking like you have a purpose."

He tried to slow down. He was more nervous than he'd thought. This might be a terrible idea, but he wasn't going to back out now.

"If you don't mind, I thought I might catch Smoke."

"Smoke? Oh, the guy who flew us back to Ventura. Oh, he's Laura Hamilton's husband."

"That's right." It was a weak excuse, and Ted knew it.

Audrey smiled. "Is he at her store? I don't mind browsing while you catch up with him."

"Thanks."

When they reached the store, he noticed his hand shaking as he opened the door for her. He hoped that he wasn't going to embarrass them both by doing this too soon. He'd talked to Ally and Brayden. He'd explained that he wasn't trying to pressure Audrey for right now, only to let her know where he hoped they were headed. Her kids had both been thrilled. Eddie and April had given him their blessing, and of course, he'd had to run it by Diego, who surprised him with his enthusiasm.

Now all the remained was to find out what Audrey thought.

Laura Hamilton greeted him with a warm smile. "Hey, Ted. Smoke's in the back. I'll go get him for you. But first, you must be Audrey? It's nice to meet you … I've heard so much about you."

"It's nice to meet you, too. I met your mom when I was here last time."

"I know, she thinks you're wonderful. Couldn't stop talking about her lovely new friend." Laura glanced at Ted. "I'll be right back." She gave him an encouraging smile before she disappeared into the back.

Audrey looked at Ted. "I love her jewelry!"

He smiled. "We should look around then."

"Oh! No. I didn't mean …"

He smiled. "At least show me what you like? I need to learn your taste." He was hoping he already had an idea of at least one piece she would love. He went over to the tray and looked at the rings.

Audrey raised her eyebrows at him.

"You don't like them?"

"Of course, I do, they're beautiful."

"Which one do you like best?"

She pointed, and he felt some of the tension ease in his shoulders. She'd chosen it!

He grinned and pulled it out of its slot.

"Do you think we should wait until she comes back?"

He shook his head with a smile and handed her the ring. "Try it on."

She took it with shaking hands and then pulled on the wire that held it to the case. Ted was relieved when the note popped out just as he'd planned.

Audrey frowned. "What's that?"

"Read it."

She picked up the note, and as she read it, the tears started to fall. He hoped with all his heart that they were happy ones.

"Will you marry me, Audrey? Please don't say no right now. I know it's too soon, and maybe it's a little too much right now. But one day, whenever you're ready," he said, speaking the words he'd memorized before he wrote them on the piece of paper she now held. "I hope with all my heart that you will say yes, to becoming my wife."

She turned to him, and her smile gave him his answer. She nodded as the tears ran down her face. "I know it's too soon, but yes, one day not too far from now."

He took the ring off the clip and slid it onto her finger. "Will you wear it until that day comes?"

Her eyes grew wide. "It's not just a prop?"

He laughed. "No! It's the one I hoped you'd choose … the one I want you to wear."

She looked at the tray and then back at him. "How did you know I'd choose this one?"

He shrugged. "We have similar tastes … and I had Laura tie the note to every ring in that tray just in case."

She laughed. "Oh, Ted!"

He closed his arms around her. "I know I said there's no rush, but any time you're ready, you just say so." Her smile faltered a little, and he understood. "In fact, scratch that. I'll ask you every Sunday if you're ready yet."

"That works."

~ ~ ~

As they walked back across the plaza, Audrey couldn't help but keep looking at her hand. The ring was so beautiful, but what it represented was even more beautiful. She knew she was the luckiest woman alive to have found Ted and to have him love her.

She looked up when she felt a spot of rain and then another. All of a sudden, it began to pour down. Ted grinned at her and pulled off his jacket. He held it up over both their heads, and they walked back to the lodge in no particular hurry.

When they reached the lobby, they were dripping wet and laughing.

"Into every life, a little rain must fall," she said.

He smiled. "We've both lived through our fair share of rain. I promise you, Audrey. I'm going to do everything in my power to give you blue skies all the way from here on out."

She smiled and touched his cheek. "I love you, Ted. And I believe you, but we both know there will always be rainy days. I'm not worried, though, because we're strong enough, and I believe our love is strong enough to see us through until the sun shines again.

He closed his arms around her, and she looped hers up around his neck, and he kissed her. Right there in the lobby with people going by, hurrying in to take shelter from the rain—as if they didn't know that into every life a little rain must fall.

She and Ted knew it. They'd each endured it, and she didn't doubt that they would face the rain again. But with him by her side she knew that the sun would always shine in her heart;

;

A Note from SJ

I hope you enjoyed Ted and Audrey's story. Please let your friends know about the books if you feel they would enjoy them as well. It would be wonderful if you would leave me a review, I'd very much appreciate it.

Check out the "Also By" page to see if any of my other series appeal to you – I have a couple of ebook freebie series starters, too, so you can take them for a test drive.

There are a few options to keep up with me and my imaginary friends:

The best way is to Sign up for my Newsletter at my website www.SJMcCoy.com. Don't worry I won't bombard you! I'll let you know about upcoming releases, share a sneak peek or two and keep you in the loop for a couple of fun giveaways I have coming up :0)

You can join my readers group to chat about the books or like my Facebook Page   www.facebook.com/authorsjmccoy
I occasionally attempt to say something in 140 characters or less(!) on Twitter

And I'm in the process of building a shiny new website at www.SJMcCoy.com

I love to hear from readers, so feel free to email me at SJ@SJMcCoy.com if you'd like. I'm better at that! :0)

I hope our paths will cross again soon. Until then, take care, and thanks for your support—you are the reason I write!

Love

SJ

PS Project Semicolon

You may have noticed that the final sentence of the story closed with a semi-colon. It isn't a typo. Project Semi Colon is a non-profit movement dedicated to presenting hope and love to those who are struggling with depression, suicide, addiction and self-injury. Project Semicolon exists to encourage, love and inspire. It's a movement I support with all my heart.

"A semicolon represents a sentence the author could have ended, but chose not to. The sentence is your life and the author is you." - Project Semicolon

This author started writing after her son was killed in a car crash. At the time I wanted my own story to be over, instead I chose to honour a promise to my son to write my 'silly stories' someday. I chose to escape into my fictional world. I know for many who struggle with depression, suicide can appear to be the only escape. The semicolon has become a symbol of support, and hopefully a reminder – Your story isn't over yet

Also by SJ McCoy

Summer Lake Silver
Clay and Marianne in Like Some Old Country Song
Seymour and Chris in A Dream Too Far
Ted and Audrey in A Little Rain Must Fall

Coming soon - Izzy and Diego in Where the Rainbow Ends

Summer Lake Seasons
Angel and Luke in Take These Broken Wings
Zack and Maria in Too Much Love to Hide
Logan and Roxy in Sunshine Over Snow
Ivan and Abbie in Chase the Blues Away
Colt and Cassie in Forever Takes a While

Summer Lake Series
Love Like You've Never Been Hurt (FREE in ebook form)
Work Like You Don't Need the Money
Dance Like Nobody's Watching
Fly Like You've Never Been Grounded
Laugh Like You've Never Cried
Sing Like Nobody's Listening
Smile Like You Mean It
The Wedding Dance
Chasing Tomorrow
Dream Like Nothing's Impossible
Ride Like You've Never Fallen
Live Like There's No Tomorrow
The Wedding Flight

Remington Ranch Series
Mason (FREE in ebook form) and also available as Audio
Shane
Carter
Beau
Four Weddings and a Vendetta

A Chance and a Hope
Chance is a guy with a whole lot of story to tell. He's part of the fabric of both Summer Lake and Remington Ranch. He needed three whole books to tell his own story.

Chance Encounter
Finding Hope
Give Hope a Chance

Love in Nashville
Autumn and Matt in Bring on the Night

The Davenports
Oscar
TJ
Reid

The Hamiltons
Cameron and Piper in Red wine and Roses
Chelsea and Grant in Champagne and Daisies
Mary Ellen and Antonio in Marsala and Magnolias
Marcos and Molly in Prosecco and Peonies
Coming Next
Grady

About the Author

I'm SJ, a coffee addict, lover of chocolate and drinker of good red wines. I'm a lost soul and a hopeless romantic. Reading and writing are necessary parts of who I am. Though perhaps not as necessary as coffee! I can drink coffee without writing, but I can't write without coffee.

I grew up loving romance novels, my first boyfriends were book boyfriends, but life intervened, as it tends to do, and I wandered down the paths of non-fiction for many years. My life changed completely a few years ago and I returned to Romance to find my escape.

I write 'Sweet n Steamy' stories because to me there is enough angst and darkness in real life. My favorite romances are happy escapes with a focus on fun, friendships and happily-ever-afters, just like the ones I write.

These days I live in beautiful Montana, the last best place. If I'm not reading or writing, you'll find me just down the road in the park - Yellowstone. I have deer, eagles and the occasional bear for company, and I like it that way :0)